JARED DETTER

The Other Side of the Door

This book is dedicated to my eldest son, Luke.

From a young age, you were intuitive and curious, which I think is a good running head start toward imagination. I hope this book helps to keep those flames burning. I can't wait to see what's in store for you.

Some day you will be old enough to start reading fairy tales again.

C.S. Lewis

Preface

When I was a child, my mother had the great idea of writing a birthday letter to each of her children each year that would encapsulate the major milestones and events from the previous year. She would include funny anecdotes and things that she wanted to preserve for posterity, such as what sports I played, who my friends were, and what I most enjoyed. When we left the house, we were given 18 unopened birthday letters that we could read through. It was really quite amazing how much would have been lost to memory without these letters.

When I got married, my wife decided to carry on this tradition with our children. I was glad of this, but I almost felt like she had taken something from my side of the family for herself, which left me wondering what I could do that was unique for each of my children. I honestly don't know where this idea came from (other than perhaps my love of reading, particularly fiction), but I decided that I was going to write a novel for each of my boys, with them being the main character in their own story.

I had never even considered writing a novel before and did not consider myself the creative writing type. However, I have this tendency of following through on things that I set my mind to, and the book in your hand (or your electronic device) is the result of that decision I made many years ago. I'm thrilled to have finally gotten this in print, not only because it's a significant accomplishment, but because now Luke has an heirloom from me that is probably one of the most unique gifts I could ever give him. I sincerely hope he enjoys it.

For those of you who know me, I have two more boys and two more books to publish. Here's to hoping I don't run out of ideas before I run out of children…

Acknowledgement

A book is never written in a vacuum. Even if one is writing in solitude, there is the ghost of every book the author has ever read that is in the room during the writing. Every life experience lingers somewhere in the author's brain. So, in a sense, every author one has read can claim some small credit for the literary output of the writer. In the same sense, there are many people who shaped the writer's life, even in small and unnoticed ways that can impact how a writer sees the world and thinks about people, relationships, and imagination.

So, let me take a moment and reflect on these. It's virtually impossible to consider the impact of all the authors I've read. As my mom likes to say, I started to read (under her tutelage) before I entered kindergarten. I saw that my older brother, Jason, was beginning to learn how to read in school, and I wanted in on the fun. After my severely negative reaction to the school recommending she not help me to read before I started school (apparently to make sure I didn't get bored and become a behavior problem), she relented and helped me learn how to read. And I've never stopped since. I honestly can't overestimate the impact that books have had on my life. I feel like I could hardly survive without them.

When I was in sixth grade, one of the books I had to read for school was C.S. Lewis' *The Lion, the Witch, and the Wardrobe*. I was generally familiar with the story, as I had seen the 1979 cartoon adaptation several times as a small child and had enjoyed it. I distinctly remember reading the book and coming to the part where Mr. Tumnus is familiarizing Lucy with the lay of the land and says, "'This is the land of Narnia', said the faun, 'where we are now; all that lies between the lamp-post and the great castle of Cair Paravel on the eastern sea.'" I remember a thrill running through me when I read 'the great castle of Cair Paravel on the eastern sea'. There was something about that clause that was magical to me and seemed full of possibilities and adventures. That phrase didn't just transport my head but my heart also. I felt a longing for what he was describing. That longing has never left me, and I still feel it every time I read that line. My love of all things C.S. Lewis began in sixth grade, and he has a bigger literary influence on me than any other author.

As I grew up and was able to tackle more complex themes and plots, I discovered J.R.R. Tolkien. As it turns out, he was good friends with C.S. Lewis, being the most famous members of the Inklings, a relatively informal group of Oxford authors, who met to discuss their writing. I remember reading the *Lord of the Rings* for the first time and being left stunned by the depth and richness of Tolkien's creation. Also, I have never read an author whose prose reads so much like poetry. He created a whole world in his books, and it's a masterpiece. And I'm one of those people who not only read the *Silmarillion* but thoroughly enjoyed it!

One more author that I'll mention who was seminal to my imagination and my interest in fantasy and historical fiction - Sir Thomas Mallory. I'm not sure where my family picked up this book, but we had an illustrated edition of Le Morte D'Arthur, the pictures coming courtesy of the great Arthur Rackham. Even though it was written in archaic English, I was entranced as a young teenager by the stories - the grand adventures, the romance of the characters, and the inevitable tragedy. Even as I'm writing this, I believe this book, perhaps more than anything else, shaped my love of the British Isles, it's medieval history, and the romance of the stories from that period. The magic of that book has never left my head.

As I've gotten older, I've found myself reading more and more historical fiction, the vast majority about the British Isles in the medieval period. This has exposed me to some of my favorite contemporary authors, who are worthy of emulating (if you're a writer) and reading (if you love to read). I recommend anyone check out the following authors: Bernard Cornwell (particularly the Saxon Tales books), Stephen Lawhead (particularly The Song of Albion trilogy), and Edoardo Albert (particularly the Northumbrian Thrones trilogy). These men have greatly encouraged my continued journey through Bookland that I started so many years ago.

Regarding the people who have shaped my love for reading and books, I must mention my parents first. Obviously, I owe a great debt of gratitude to my mother, who did not follow the recommendation of the grade school, and she dedicated time to teaching me to read. I'm so grateful for this head start. Not only this, but she would read to me as a child as well, which does wonders for the imagination. My father provided a household that never lacked for books. He has enjoyed reading for as long as I can remember, which meant it took little convincing to make sure I had books of my own. Even to this day, I love talking books with my dad. The last person I'll mention is my first grade teacher, Miss Lewis. She happened to come along at the right time when I was hitting my stride as a reader, and I loved the reading assignments she gave us. In addition, I still remember hanging on every word when she read to the class a book called *The Christmas Duck*. Years later, I found the book online, bought it, and I have it to this day. There was something about her style as a teacher that I think helped my reading take flight that year. She got married after the end of the school year, changed her last name, and left the school. I have no idea where she is or what her last name is now, but I'm grateful for her contribution at the right time to my love of reading.

Regarding this book, I'd like to thank Luke for being born - otherwise I never would have written this. Additionally, I'd like to specifically thank my wife, Rachel, both of my parents (Al and Marie), and my friends Kevin Baldizon and Edoardo Albert, all of whom gave selflessly of their time to read my drafts and give valuable editorial comments. Without their support, this book wouldn't be what it is now. I'd also like to gratefully thank those of who you supported me through Kickstarter, which allowed me to ultimately get this published. In particular, I'd like to thank Jason & Beth Detter, Al & Marie Detter, Jan Luke, Mike Barbee, Corey Baechel, Dan & Stephanie Seltzer, Jacob & Nicole Mauer, Tracey Drake, Mona Martin, Kelly & Monique Chestnut, and Ellen Pilcher for their generous crowdfunding donations that truly went above and beyond. Your contribution means more than you know. Lastly, I'd like to thank all the readers who took the time to pick up this book. Because what is a book without a reader? I sincerely hope you enjoy it!

1

The Living House

The small valley was shrouded in so much mist that Luke could only see several feet in front of him. So thick was this blanket that it dampened all sound, the dew on the grass wetting his bare feet. The air was chill, but Luke was not cold. Although he was in a strange place, he showed no awareness of it. Luke registered no fear. He lacked even the basic self-awareness to wonder why he found himself outside without shoes, apparently lost.

He began to walk slowly, cautiously, through the mist. The soft grass gave way beneath him, the dew coating his feet. Trance-like, measured steps carried him toward some unknown destination. An unconscious influence was patiently pulling Luke toward its discovery.

Moving through the fog, Luke became aware that the terrain around him was beginning to slope slowly uphill. The valley floor began to rise, bearing him higher and higher. The gentle slope turned into a modest incline, eventually progressing into a moderately difficult climb. The slippery grass made Luke stumble on several occasions. Dropping to his knees, he used his hands to grasp the grass, pulling himself forward, drenching his hands in the process. He traveled several minutes in this manner, slowly crawling up the hill, making difficult, but steady, headway. Eventually, he came to a flat parcel of ground where he stopped to orient himself.

For the first time since the beginning of his short journey, Luke began to wonder where he was. In fact, it struck him as odd that he had not considered this before. Maybe it was his panting for breath, his dirty hands, or his wet clothes, moistened by the dew on his climb, that brought him back to awareness. He could not remember how he had gotten here, nor had he any explanation for the situation in which he found himself. There was only a vague sense that he was 'supposed to' head in the direction that he had chosen. Strangely enough, despite his increasing self-awareness, he still felt no fear.

He plopped down on the wet grass to collect his thoughts and formulate a plan, when he noticed that the mist was less dense at this height than it was below. He could see across the valley and discerned the edge of a wood a little distance from the base of the hill he had just climbed. The rest of the wood trailed away into the distance and was obscured in the fog. He could see little else, although he began to hear what sounded like waves crashing onto a shore a short way off.

He stood to resume his exploration, using the sound of the waves to help him stay oriented in the fog. Turning around, he was surprised to see a large building that he had not noticed before, only a short distance in front of him. As he cautiously approached it, Luke surmised that the building was actually a house, albeit a unique house. As the mist lifted, more and more details of the building became visible, tugging at Luke's curiosity.

The house was roughly square and appeared to have a very ancient foundation of stacked field stone. The stone looked sturdy and uncompromised by the years, but the growth of moss and lichen spoke of its age. The earthy tones of green, brown, and gray upon the stones gave him the impression that the foundation of the house had simply risen out of the hill. Upon this foundation were robust looking walls made of large, gray limestone blocks. The solid look and regular pattern of the stone and mortar gave Luke the feeling that the walls were erected sometime during the medieval period, vaguely reminding him of castle walls. The roof was pitched and made of gray slate. A mossy substance was growing on the roof and in between the stones in the wall, further adding to the impression of age. Small windows flanked each side of the main entrance, but the windows were black, as if no light could penetrate the interior. Despite the obvious age of the house and its apparent desertion, it presented itself as solid and structurally sound.

This ancient house captivated Luke and pulled him toward it. He approached with curiosity, studying the lines of the house. The square structure was interrupted only on the corner nearest to him, where the stone fanned out into a protruding rounded shape, which looked like a miniature castle tower.

He paused before the house to reassess his surroundings, now that the fog had all but disappeared. Luke could now see an ocean in the distance that was making the ceaseless, rhythmic sound of waves that he had heard earlier. Resplendent sunshine was emerging from the fog, sprinkling the waves with its radiance. Under normal circumstances, Luke would have made the short walk to explore the shoreline that was hidden beyond the hill. But these were not normal circumstances.

The forest at the foot of the valley was also now clearly visible. Its lush green and brown were a testament to the health of the land. The trees spread, thousands upon thousands, the forest trailing off in the distance and toward the ocean. Separated from the ocean by the forest, a meadow established the eastern border of the trees, spilling out into the valley below. Long green grass swayed in the meadow, accented by varicolored wildflowers and purple heather in full bloom. A more picture-perfect scene is rarely found, and this was not lost on Luke. Several moments passed as he drank in his surroundings, grateful for the disappearance of the fog and the emergence of the lovely green valley and its forest, caressed by the sounds of the ocean.

Despite the hypnotic influence the scenery exerted, the curious house played at the fringes of Luke's mind until he turned to face it again. An aged wooden door, placed in an arching frame of grey stone blocks, highlighted the front of the structure. A large, white capstone finished the arch above the door, crowning the guardian of the house, through which all would pass who wanted to gain entrance. As he approached the doorway, the capstone of the arch began to change. The stone began to glow, emanating a warm, yellow luminescence, accentuated by the sharply defined appearance of strange runes, which seemed to glow white-hot.

Excitement began to pulse inside of Luke. There was no way of knowing what message lay in the runes or what it might portend, but it was drawing him to enter. An iron ring hung on the door, and he grasped it with both hands and gave a confident pull. The door swung open with surprising ease, allowing passage into the house. As Luke crossed the threshold, a tingling sensation pulsed through him. Pausing for a moment just inside, he let his eyes adjust to the half-light of the room. Luke was amazed by what he saw.

The room, which probably would have served as a large greeting room, appeared to be a living forest. The forest, however, seemed to be a planned part of the room's appointments. The flooring was made of flagstone with rich, black soil packed in between the stones. Small saplings appeared here and there, bent into the approximate shape of furniture. Just to his left, Luke noticed a pair of saplings growing so close together that they wound delicately around each other up to the height of the middle of his thigh. The leaves at the top grew in a thick, flat, and surprisingly circular shape, giving the impression of a small, decorative table. A series of low, green shrubs seemed to grow into one another, forming the likeness of a chaise lounge. Stumps of large trees were scattered about the room, with a hollowed-out portion of the tree remaining, bearing a resemblance to large, high-backed chairs. The large beams in the walls appeared to be alive, sprouting rather thick, strong branches reaching upward, seemingly supporting the uppermost part of the house. A thick canopy of leaves served as a ceiling, creating a continuous blanket of green above him. Green and brown moss grew in several areas of the floor, creating beautiful area rugs, unrivaled in their thickness.

Wandering silently around the room, Luke noticed a little stream that began in the center of the floor and disappeared under the back wall. He stooped down and placed his hand in the clear, cool stream bubbling from the floor. He cupped both hands, dipped them into the water and lifted the liquid to his mouth. The water ran deliciously down his throat, cooling him as it went. The small drink invigorated him. He felt more awake, stronger, and more vital than he had ever felt in his life. He ran his fingers slowly along the moss that grew on the flagstone beside the stream. It was soft to the touch, almost velvety in its texture. He stood up and touched a leaf from a large branch protruding from the nearest wall. The leaf was of an unfamiliar shape and was a vivid shade of green. Its waxy texture and flexibility eradicated any doubt that the room was indeed alive.

Luke was overwhelmed by the wonder of this place. How could it be alive? Who could have shaped these plants to resemble furniture? These questions and many more flitted through his mind as he sat down on the thick moss, feeling its texture with his fingers. He listened to the trickle of the stream and the soft gurgling of its source, overawed by the improbable sylvan scene in the entry room of this strange, ancient house.

He might have stayed lost in his reverie indefinitely, had he not noticed that vine covered tree branches were clustering on the back wall and seemed to form a natural arbor that led from the room. He stood up and let his fingers trail along the wooden and leafy wall as he made his way to the arbor. Once there, he spread apart the vines that hung down, revealing a rather ordinary looking hallway. The walls were made of the same gray stone as the outside of the house, and the flagstone floor extended the length of the hallway, making a passage to four rooms, two on each side of the passage. The hallway was completely clear of any decoration on the walls and contained no furniture. The rooms off this hall seemed to encompass the remainder of the house.

As Luke continued, he noticed that three of the four doors were rather ornate, made from wood carved in themed patterns, and were beautiful to behold. The last doorway on the right was plain and smallish and was made from rough-hewn boards without decoration. It was humble-looking and rounded at the top, unlike the other three others in the hallway, which were rectangular.

Opposite the plain door was one intricately carved with patterns that reminded Luke of the sea. The moon and the stars were carved at the top and spilled into constellations that framed the edge of the entire door. A ship rode the crest of waves on an ocean, broken only by land in the distance. The carvings were of incredible quality and comprised the entire top half of the door. He chose to enter this room first.

As soon as Luke opened the door, his senses were bombarded by the sound of the ocean, seagulls, and the smell of salty air. He cautiously stepped into the room to survey his surroundings. The floor was hard and made of uniform planks of wood. In the center of the room was a thick pillar that rose from the floor and disappeared into the ceiling. Directly in front of him, the room formed a raised platform flanked with railings, creating what looked like the bow of a ship. The railing was about four feet high, and the sky was deep blue above it. Behind him, the door through which he had just entered now seemed to lead back into a small ship's cabin.

Luke walked toward the railing to peer over. What he saw astonished him. Below was the ocean, and Luke felt for the first time the gentle rock of the boat on which he found himself. In the distance he could see land and the spray of the surf as the waves washed onto the shore. Seagulls squawked on the breeze that was ruffling his hair. He reached out over the railing and felt his hand smack against the wall. The realism of the room stood in stark contrast to the evidence felt with his hand, that the scene was unfolding on two-dimensional walls. His environs looked as real as if he had been standing on an actual ship.

The sound of the waves and the warmth of the sun had a relaxing effect, lulling Luke into relishing the wonders of the sea room a while longer. Once he had determined that the room was indeed enclosed by four solid walls Luke's mind turned toward what he might discover in the other rooms. As he paused in the doorway, Luke glanced back into the room, and it appeared a world of its own within the confines of four incredible walls.

Luke hoped that the other doorway on this side of the hall might provide an extension to the room he had just left. This hope was not fulfilled as he walked up the corridor, however, as the door was scored with vastly different carvings than the previous one.

Luke traced the outline of a castle with knights on the lawn in the foreground. On the left-hand side of the castle stood a tower, bringing his mind back to the short tower on the front left of the house in which he stood. The sun stood high in the sky, as the medieval reverie unfolded on the door. A forest flanked the castle, and a hunting party looked to be setting off with a pack of dogs. Tents were pitched, each with a banner above it unfurled in the wind. As with the previous door, the scene covered the entire top half of the door, the skill of the artist conveying a scene reminiscent of Camelot.

Opening the door, the room was largely circular with a conical ceiling, reaching nearly fifteen feet above the floor, which was solid and cold on his bare feet. The stone in the floor was less forgiving than the wooden planks from the room in which he had just departed. The room contained few appointments, save a blackened fireplace, over which hung a faded tapestry portraying a medieval hunt, a small chest against the wall, a large rug in the center of the room, an empty four-post bed, and a narrow, double-arched window cut into the curved, stone wall opposite the door.

Luke walked slowly toward the window, unsure what he would see. A pale moon shone through, and its blue light fell onto the ornate and thickly woven rug in the center of the room. He crossed it on his way to the window and marveled at its intricacy. Largely green and brown, it was marked with traditional Celtic patterns, weaving and dancing in and out of one another, never truly beginning or ending. The skill needed to create such a rug would have undoubtedly made this an expensive acquisition.

He reached the window and gazed at the landscape. The valley sprawled out below him, stretching toward the forest. The moonlight that illuminated the landscape stood in stark contrast to the morning sunshine he had left behind when he entered the house. He was also surprised to see that the room was no longer at ground level. Rather, he found himself gazing at the dark lawn, thirty or forty feet below the window.

Luke attempted to put his hand out of the glassless window to feel the cool night air. As with the first room, he could not extend his hand through the window, his hand striking an invisible wall. The vision of the land outside the window was inaccessible. He gazed once more at the serenity of the valley below before turning around to explore the room.

The walls were made of the same material as the floor, rising in well-laid stone all around him. His eyes traced the walls from top to bottom, pulling his attention to the old, ornate chest against the wall a short way off. Thick strips of brass, fortifying the exposed wood, bound the chest. Leather handles were on the left and right sides, fastened to the chest with brass clamps. Luke's attempts to open the chest failed, as an ancient iron lock secured it from unwanted intruders. The cold fireplace offered no warmth to battle the chilly night breeze wafting through the window.

Luke returned to the relative warmth of the hallway, wanting to explore the rooms on the other side of the hall. An examination of the door directly across from the one he had just exited revealed a small building that was surrounded by quaint little gardens and a crudely made stone half-wall. The building was rectangular and had the look of a tiny chapel with a small addition on one side, having a separate entrance. This scene was surrounded by religious symbols, which bordered the door. He was unsure of the significance of some of these symbols, but he recognized a few, particularly a cross, which appeared at regular intervals amongst the rest.

He pressed open this door to find himself in the building depicted in the quaint scene on the door. It led him in to a very small and dimly lit room, with scarcely anything in it other than a bed and a small table with a rough chair next to it. The table and chair were located under the solitary window, adding light to several dim candles. These candles illuminated a coarse sheet of parchment and a quill pen placed neatly beside them on the table.

There was a rough-hewn door on the wall opposite him. Luke moved to see where the door led but was once again preempted from satisfying his curiosity by the wall. The door was part of the illusion and could not be reached nor opened. He sidled to the solitary window in the room, supporting his weight on the table as he leaned toward the scene in front of him. A pleasant, if somewhat overgrown, lawn presented itself, bisected by a path that led from the larger portion of the building out to a small, half-wall with an opening through which the path passed. The wall was bordered on the inside with neatly kept beds of wildflowers. Seeing no other exit from the room, he turned and strode out the door, which led him back into the hallway.

There, Luke made for the last, and least interesting, door, on the same side of the hallway as the room he had just left. The carvings on the other doors had offered some clue as to what might lie behind them. This one did not. He hesitated before entering to consider the significance of this seemingly out of place and unimpressive entrance into the final room. Reaching out for the handle on the door, Luke paused momentarily, suddenly unsure if he should proceed, the door giving him no clue what might lie beyond. He reached out again and grasped the handle of the door, only to find it locked.

2

By Way of Introduction

Luke Detter was in that phase of life where boyhood was wearing off and manhood was setting in, and vestiges of both could be seen juxtaposed with each other. He was of average build with dark hair and pleasing features. He lived in typical American suburbia, enjoying the comfort of the upper middle-class life that his parents afforded him. He was the only child of two early middle-aged parents, who loved him very much.

Luke's father, Alan, worked in middle management for a publishing house that had offices in both America and England. He had, in fact, been working in England when Luke was born. They had moved to the United States at a time in Luke's life when no memories of England could possibly follow him across the ocean to America. Alan was a hard-working individual who tried his best to provide for his family, even if it meant the possibility of another move, uprooting the family from the place that they had lived for more than a decade.

Luke's mother, Catherine, was a gentle woman who had worked as a receptionist at a local business ever since Luke was old enough to go to school. Despite working outside of the home, she prided herself on being there for Luke whenever he needed her. She was loving, but not doting, and her small family was the most important thing in her life. She would do what it took to be supportive, even if it meant leaving the familiar behind.

* * *

Luke awoke from a dream-filled sleep - a dream that was both rather striking and mysterious, although the details seemed to be chased from his consciousness by the bright morning sunshine flooding into his room. He had just gotten out of school for the summer and was taking full advantage of the opportunity to sleep in. He sat up in bed, rubbed his eyes, and swung his feet around to rest them on the floor. Gazing contentedly around his room, he looked forward to the possibilities of a young summer. But before these possibilities could be fully explored, he would need to eat.

With the thought of breakfast crowding his teenage mind, he bound down the stairs, grabbing the already loose railing to help him navigate the turn in the stairwell. *I can't get away with that much more. I'm gonna break that railing, and mom's gonna kill me,* he thought. He did not contemplate this long, however, as his mind turned quickly back to his gnawing stomach. After dismounting the stairs, Luke headed for the kitchen, mentally working through the culinary options that might satisfy his morning hunger. He turned the corner to the kitchen and stopped, surprised at what he saw.

"Dad, what are you doing home? I thought you'd be at work by now. It's after 9:30."

Alan answered after swallowing a mouthful of scrambled eggs. "Son, I decided to stay home today. There has been something in the works with my job, and your mom and I did not want to say anything to you until it was final."

"You didn't get fired, did you Dad?" Luke asked.

"No, Luke, it's a little different. We're going home."

Luke was a little confused. "We are home. What are you talking about?"

He began, "Luke, I think you'll remember that you were born in England. I've been given a promotion at the publishing house, and they'd like to move me back to England to head a large branch over there." He absently pushed his eggs around on his plate, indicating his nervousness at how his son might respond.

Luke planted his feet and put his hands on his hips, almost in defiance. "Dad,

I sure hope you're kidding. This is the only place that I know. I don't know England. I don't care about England. My friends are here. Everything I care about is here. Does Mom know about this?" he asked, almost in accusation.

At that moment, Catherine entered the kitchen, the timing a little suspicious. "Honey, your father and I have discussed this. As you know, your father is from here in America, but England is where I grew up. That's where *my* family is from. It would be a great opportunity to travel the world, to see different things, and to broaden your horizons. I really think that you're going to like it over there."

Luke stood in stunned silence. He knitted his brows and shifted his weight back and forth before finally asking, "Are you asking how I feel about the possibility, or are you telling me what your decision is?"

"Well, Luke, we're not so much informing you of *our* decision as much as letting you know what the company has decided. They could really use me over there, and I'm not in a position to say no. This is a great opportunity for our family, our finances, and my career. This is the reality of the business, and I think that we'll really enjoy the chance we're being given."

"So that's it then. Just pick up and move across the ocean. Just like that, leaving everything behind I've ever known."

"I know it's a lot to process," his mother replied softly. "It'll be a big change for all of us." She wisely refrained from trying any further to convince him this was the right course of action.

"I've got to be alone for a little while," was all Luke would allow himself to say before turning on his heels and walking out the front door.

"Well, I think that could have gone worse," Alan said dryly.

"I knew this would be hard for him. He doesn't really know anything other than this. It is a tough time of life for him to be moving," Catherine said as she slowly paced in the kitchen. "He's a good kid, though, and I'm sure that he'll adapt just fine. I guess I'm really not that worried about him, although I wish we could have prepared him better."

"I know. I just didn't want to upset him with something that might not have happened. I wanted to know for sure before we told him. I just wish we had more time before the move, but moving in the summer works so much better for us as a family." He paused for a moment before continuing, "Well, I better head off to work. I'm going to clear out my desk and bring everything home, so that we can be prepared for the movers next week."

As the conversation was wrapping up in the kitchen, Luke was already heading toward his favorite spot. There was a rather lonely road near his home that led to some woods, covering several dozen acres. It was someplace that he always went when he felt like being alone. It had helped him many times when he needed to work through some emotions or spend some time alone in thought. Today, he needed it more than ever.

He spied the little trail that led through the long grass and weeds that bordered the woods and marked the way into the interior. As he entered the tree line, he followed the narrow trail past the big, twisted oak tree, where he always jumped to touch its lowest branches. On this morning, he walked by the tree without noticing it. He followed the path to the little stream, lightly stepping across it, going deeper into the woods.

His favorite spot was about a quarter mile in where a small waterfall fell from a rock ledge eight feet high, creating a pleasant cascade of water and sound that was always soothing to Luke. The tall trees were thick in this spot, but there was a break in the canopy that let in enough light to illuminate the area around the waterfall. At this time of day, the sun was peeking through the opening, casting its rays on the water, making the rushing water sparkle with the light of thousands of shimmering diamonds.

Despite his troubles, the scene made him relax. He could always be moved by beauty, and this spot was beautiful to him. Standing near the base of the waterfall, it was impossible to see its source. Luke liked to imagine that the waterfall just sprang from the rock, spilling its life-giving issue to the stream below. The stream was only about five feet across and about two feet deep. However, time and the workings of the waterfall had created a small, clear pool at the bottom of the cascade. Across from the waterfall and facing toward the pool was a strange, chair-like rock formation upon which he would frequently sit to take in this treasured scene and think. It was this seat that Luke sought that summer morning to think about how his life would soon be changing, and how little control he had over his circumstances.

Luke had been sitting on the stone a short while before he was lulled into a sleep by the sun's warm rays and the gentle rush of the waterfall and gurgle of the stream, as it wound away into the woods. He seamlessly slipped into a dream, the vividness of which kept this truth from Luke.

He found himself alone in a valley. Behind him was a deep forest, spreading out for miles across the country. Somewhere off to his left, he could hear the sounds of the surf, pounding the shores. In front of him was a hill. Atop this hill stood a house, a very strange house, but it had an air of familiarity about it. In fact, this whole place looked familiar. It slowly dawned upon Luke that he had been here before, and rather recently. He could not place how he had gotten here and why he had been here before. Luke vaguely remembered the area being shrouded in fog, but today, the sun was high in the sky and the air was clear. He decided to traverse the hill and enter the house. There was a vague feeling that this would not be his first time inside the house, but he could not remember any details of the original experience.

He was about to climb the hill, when from behind him, he heard a faint voice whispering, "Do not forget." He quickly spun around in the direction of the voice but saw no one. He saw no movement in the forest, and there was no evidence that anyone had been behind him. He went up the hill, looking back over his shoulder several times on the way, seeing nothing that would indicate the presence of anyone other than himself. By the time he reached the summit, he had convinced himself that what he had heard was only a figment of his imagination.

The view opened wide from the top of the hill. The ocean lay on his left in the distance. The sweep of the ocean gracefully curved inland along the coast for several miles, reaching its greatest penetration a short walk from where he stood. Farther still, the land swept back out into the ocean, making a crescent-shaped shoreline with the middle arching inland. Luke approached the house and paused before it to reacquaint himself with its construction. Its seeming antiquity amazed him, especially the foundations, and the circular, tower-looking portion of the house captured his imagination. He stopped before the front doorway, as a sound caught his attention. The faint words of a whisper seemed to be riding on the wind, "Do not forget." The words gave him pause for just a moment before he quickly reached for the door to step inside.

He found himself startled awake by his own movement as he was reclining upon the rock. He had reached out his hand during the dream, shaking him from his sleep. He vaguely remembered dreaming about a picturesque valley and a strange house, but this was rapidly pushed from his memory by the thought of the major life change that would soon descend upon his family, taking him to a wholly unfamiliar country across the Atlantic Ocean.

* * *

It was evening before Luke returned home. His parents had not yet become concerned, as they knew Luke to be level-headed. They allowed him the space that he needed to digest the news he had received that morning. They also knew that Luke wouldn't just sit and simmer, nursing his grievances. He would use to the time to process his feelings and start working through what he needed to do to prepare himself for the biggest change of his life.

Luke returned home quietly, pausing at the front door before going inside. He made sure that no one was in the living room, giving him free access to the stairs. He went straight to his room without speaking to his parents. Luke was still processing the change that was upon him and did not want to interact with anyone until he was more settled in his spirit. His parents spoke quietly down in the kitchen.

"How do you think he's taking it?" asked Catherine.

"I'm not sure. I would imagine that he's a little upset, but he's a good kid. Luke's got a good head on his shoulders, and he's always responded well to challenges." Alan continued, "I think he'll be all right in the morning...I hope".

"I hope so too," she added. "Luke was so young when we moved to the United States. He doesn't remember anything of England. For me, it's going home, and you lived there long enough to know what you're getting into. He's got nothing over there."

Alan paused for a moment, thinking, before he responded, "I wouldn't say that he's got nothing over there. He was born there. He doesn't really know your family, but there are the strange circumstances with his adoption…"

She didn't let him finish, "Sssshhh. Don't speak so loudly," she said in a raspy whisper. "I don't want him to hear us talking about this. It would be too much change for him all at once. I know we should have told him earlier about his adoption, but I don't think now is a great time to break our silence."

"I know. Now's not the time, but just the same, I think there's something to the items that came with him in the adoption that might help us find out more information." He paused for a moment in thought. "Well, we can talk more about this in the morning. It's getting late, and we haven't accomplished much today. We've got a lot of work in front of us before we're settled in a home again."

They spent the next several hours packing various household items and discussing what was yet to be accomplished before the work of moving out of their longtime home was completed. While they were engaged in this process, Luke was in his room struggling to come to terms with the loss of his life as he knew it. He wasn't planning the move from their house, as his parents were. He was planning how he would break this difficult news to his friends and how he would say goodbye. He was lamenting the loss of the familiar things around him – things that he had taken for granted as always being with him. Soon they would be gone, and he would have to forge a new life from the ashes of his old one. He had never felt loss this like before and wasn't sure how to manage the grief that was welling up inside his chest. He wanted to rage against his parents, but he was wise enough to know that anger wasn't his problem now. It was the heavy, hollow feeling in his chest that he was afraid would never go away. He felt like he could cry, but there were no tears – just the cavernous hole of loss weighing him down.

After wrapping up for the evening, both of Luke's parents went upstairs, pausing briefly in front of Luke's closed door. The silence prompted them to continue toward their bedroom. If they had waited around a short while longer, they might have heard restless movement and sleepy, muffled words coming from Luke's room - something about woods, a hill, and a strange house.

3

Coming to England

The tedium of the long flight across the Atlantic went unnoticed by Luke; he was lost in thought for most of the trip. The initial shock of the move had worn off, but it had been a struggle for Luke to reach some measure of peace about his situation. He had said goodbye to his friends and grieved the loss of his boyhood home and his place of solitude in the woods. Closure in these areas, however, was not enough to explain the peace that had lately descended upon Luke during this time of change. In fact, the morning of the flight he seemed to have accepted his fate rather well.

As his parents were nestled together, reclining in their coach-fare seats napping quietly, Luke was sorting through his thoughts, trying to sequence together the series of dreams that had haunted him, beginning even before hearing about the move to England. For some reason, these dreams appeared in amazing clarity but seemed to fade into the fog of semi-consciousness upon waking. He was increasingly confident that he had put together the basic details of the rather consistent dreams, and he had a strange feeling that it was important that he not forget them.

These he recorded, dredged from his memory, "I always begin in a pleasant valley… forest behind me and to one side…appears to be an ocean or rather large body of water to the other…always compelled to go up the hill in front of me…odd house at the top with strange figures carved in stone above doorway…possibly words? Inside of the house seems to be doorways to other places…each room seems to be a separate place. Room 1: a forest…plants apparently alive and growing…stream in room. Room 2: seem to be on a ship out on the ocean…is a cabin on board but end up in hallway when I try to go inside. Room 3: is this part of a castle? Seems to be medieval…a rather interesting room. Room 4: might be an ancient country church…a small scantly furnished living space…quaint gardens. Room 5: have never gotten into this room. Dream usually seems to end here…Doubtful this room is as interesting as the others, if door is any indication."

He reread his notes several times, content with the description, feeling that he had done justice to the basic themes in the dream. He was unsure of the importance of the details, but he felt much better once they had been written down and removed from being the sole property of his memory. Although the rest of the flight was monotonous, thoughts of his new life surged through his head, as he wondered what the days ahead would have in store.

* * *

They landed without incident and shuffled through the vastness of humanity coursing through London's Heathrow airport. After navigating their way through the labyrinthine halls of the sprawling airport, they found their luggage, and made their way to the car waiting for them, which had been provided by the publishing company. These were Luke's first steps in his new country, but it didn't feel like home. He hoped his new life in England didn't match the sensory confusion and insignificance he felt now among this sea of humans, thousands walking by without seeming to notice him. After exiting the airport, they were met by an intern from the company whose assignment that day was to convey Luke's family from the airport to their temporary living quarters near the coast, east of London.

They placed their luggage in the trunk and entered the car. Luke wondered at the fact that the steering wheel was on the opposite side than in America and that the vehicles occupied the left-hand lane. This curiosity occupied much of his attention at first, especially while traversing the streets of the outskirts of western London. But as the driver pulled onto the motorway to avoid the press of driving through the city, Luke's thoughts turned inward, the endless cars and nondescript roadside scenery failing to capture his attention.

As they left the motorway and drove into more captivating environs, he peered at the landscape with much interest as they drove along. It was beautiful, he thought, not unlike what one might see in parts of the United States, but somehow more quaint, more antique, and everything was green. He watched as the farmland, hills, and centuries old buildings passed before his eyes while the miles in front of them fell away, and they approached their destination.

"You know that you were born in England, don't you sweetie?" asked Catherine.

"I remember you telling me that, but I obviously don't remember anything else. How old did you say that I was when we came to America?"

"You were about six months old when we made the flight across the Atlantic, bringing you to America, much too young to remember anything of England." She paused for a moment, as if lost in the past. "I can't believe that we are actually here!" she said, shaking off the reverie. "I've told you many times that I grew up in England, and it's so good to be back. In a way, it's like coming home."

"You know," noted Luke, "I never really wondered this before, but now that I'm in the country of my birth, where was I born? What part of England did I come from, and are we going to be anywhere near it?"

Luke's parents glanced at each other a little nervously, but Luke was peering out the window at the passing countryside and missed the subtle exchange.

Alan broke the momentary silence. "How long before we get to the house?"

"It's just about a mile down the road," said the intern. "I have a car at the house to take back to work, and I've been instructed to leave this for your use as a company car."

At this, Luke's parents fell into conversation reviewing the plans for the rest of the evening. They were relieved that this discussion was not interrupted by any further questions from Luke, hoping that his query would fade from memory. Just a few moments later, the car turned into a circular gravel driveway in front of a quaint Tudor-style cottage that was to be occupied by Luke and his family until they found suitable housing for long-term use. The car came to a halt and Luke was the first one out. The intern opened the trunk; Luke grabbed his parcels and followed the intern into the cottage.

The house was evidently old, possibly several centuries had come and gone since it was first raised on its foundation. It left the impression that, despite its age, the place was well cared for. Entering through the front door, Luke stepped into the left end of a small sitting room.

The sitting room had low ceilings and hardwood floors. The wood used in the floors was of a rough grain but kept clean and polished as well as could be. The walls were of plaster and appeared to have been recently whitewashed and were interrupted only by the front leaded glass windows and doors directly to the left and straight ahead on the opposite wall. Upon the walls hung attractive paintings of the English countryside. A small fireplace was located in the center of the opposite wall, lying cold and empty, due to the pleasantly warm summer day. A portrait of an unknown man hung upon the brick above the fireplace. A large area rug occupied the floor in front of the hearth. Upon the rug and near the fireplace was an older but clean love seat, a small coffee table bordered in a semi-circle by several wooden chairs, and a side table large enough to support a lamp to illuminate the room after sundown. Hot tea was waiting for them upon the coffee table and its smell filled the mid-afternoon air.

The intern began introducing the house. "As I'm sure you know from your correspondence with the company, this cottage is yours for up to three weeks, at which time further arrangements can be made if adequate housing has not been procured. You will have full rights to the house and the grounds during this time and you should not be disturbed other than by the presence of the gardener and a launderer who comes twice a week to clean any soiled clothes and linens. Otherwise, the house is yours to use as you see fit, providing the place is respected, as I'm sure you understand."

They were led through the sitting room to the door on the opposite wall into a kitchen. The kitchen had not been updated much in the last half-century and was rather attractive in its antiquity. There was an aged table in the center of the room, surrounded by four chairs. Atop the table was a faded cloth, upon which an attractive vase of flowers was placed. On the far wall was another table, although smaller and scarred. It gave the appearance of one used for the purpose of food preparation, next to which was located a short icebox. On the other side of the preparation table was a sink and several cupboards, presumably holding dishes, possibly functioning as a pantry as well. A wood-burning stove served the dual purpose of cooking food and heating the room on nights when a chill descended upon the countryside. The stove was piped into the chimney and looked like it had been well used over the years. Several square windows looked out onto the hills behind the kitchen, allowing ample natural light into the room.

The intern continued his speech. "This kitchen is somewhat different than what you have known, I'm sure, but it is clean, and please use it as necessary. There is also a small pub just a few miles down the road that serves very good mutton, if you're interested."

From a door on the left, they were led into the sole bedroom of the cottage. The bedroom was rather small, having only an old dresser, a bed, a cot for Luke's use, and a desk. Despite being small and affording only the necessities, the place was clean and, on the whole, looked to be adequate for short-term use.

"I know it's rather small, but we've provided a cot for Master Luke's use, and we hope you'll find the bed comfortable, sir," nodding in the direction of Alan as he finished the statement.

Attached to this room was a small addition where a former enterprising owner of the cottage decided to add a washroom, which contained all the necessities for proper toilet. They set down their baggage in the bedroom and were shown the final room of the cottage. It was adjoined to the bedroom and the sitting room and could be accessed from both.

Luke was fascinated with this final room. It appeared to serve the purpose of a reading room and seemed to impress a wholly different era of history into his mind. A well-worn, but apparently well-made, desk was placed on the wall facing the front of the house underneath a large, paned window. Through this, Luke sighted the car on the gravel driveway, and, to the right, sitting just off the driveway, the car of the intern awaiting its owner's return. Upon this desk were several books, a gas lamp, and a half-melted candle in a candlestick. Massive old bookshelves lined the walls, covered with antique books and manuscripts. Some of the books were upright, some piled in stacks, but none of the bookshelves appeared disheveled. The walls contained several large maps, some of the entire country, some of the county, and some of the surrounding small towns. All of them were carefully framed, in order to delay any further efforts of the hands of time. Luke imagined a happy old Englishman poring over his books by candlelight on a warm summer evening, renewing his aging mind through the wonderful magic of books.

"This room has been left largely untouched for the past hundred years or so. You will notice no modern amenities in here. The grandson of the original owner was quite a book lover and had pulled together a rather impressive collection of local lore and history, and we keep the room largely undisturbed. Feel free to peruse the books, but take especial care to preserve them."

The intern, referencing the hour and his need to return to work before going home, pulled Luke's focus from the wonderful details of the room. He exited the reading room, progressed into the sitting room and took a quick right out the front door. A few seconds later, his car roared to life and slowly rolled down the gravel lane and off into the distance. Luke followed out the door shortly after to survey the grounds surrounding the cottage.

Pausing for a moment in front of the building, Luke noticed the late afternoon sun, causing the shadows to creep across the ground and give the surrounding hillside a more dramatic appearance. The cottage cast a shadow on the ground, darkening a portion of a rather busy flowerbed that surrounded the house. This bed was filled with flowers in full bloom - roses, primroses, cosmos, pansies, and lupines, and dotted with shrubs, mostly hydrangea, rhododendron, and azalea, complimented by patches of ivy and wisteria that were creeping up the face of the cottage. The plants in the beds were vibrant, fed by the regular English rain, and added much to the pleasing look of the place.

Away from the cottage, the flowerbeds abruptly stopped and turned into a rolling green lawn that wrapped around the house and blended seamlessly with the surrounding hills. Here and there were patches of trees dotting the landscape, providing variation in the attractive plot upon which the cottage sat.

All this Luke took in during a short walk around the property. Having satisfied his curiosity, Luke headed back inside, wondering about dinner. After finishing a few necessary settling-in tasks, the family drove down the lane half an hour later, ready to take in both the local food and flavor at the pub.

"I think it's kind of nice. What about you, son?" asked Alan.

"I think it's great. I don't know that I'd want to stay there forever, but that cottage has so much character. I love its look and feel, and I can't wait to get at some of those books in the drawing room."

"I'm glad you like it. Your mother and I have some business to take care of at my new office tomorrow, signing papers, a few orientation meetings, and things like that. You may want to hang around here and explore a bit, what do you think?"

"I'd love to. I'm sure that I can keep myself busy."

By this time, they had settled around a wooden table in the local pub and began to look at a menu. "What are apple bangers and mash?" Luke asked with an eyebrow raised.

"Order it and see; you'll like it," Catherine encouraged. "That's one thing that you'll have to learn. The lingo is a bit different around here with food than in America. It won't take long to adjust."

They ordered their food and enjoyed the local atmosphere in their new hometown. They happily bantered about the cottage and their new life. Their dinner was soon brought to the table and the family happily busied themselves eating their fill and preparing to turn in early for the evening.

4

The Gardener

Morning came, and Luke's parents were gone before he woke for the day. He roused himself out of the cot and went into the kitchen to see if he could find himself a passable breakfast. He rummaged through the cupboards, found some fresh bread, no doubt purchased for their arrival, located the toaster and started to toast the bread. In the icebox, he found some butter and jelly, which he spread generously on his toast. A glass jar of fresh milk also awaited him. While breakfasting at the kitchen table, he saw a note written in his mother's hand. It explained his parents' desire to let him have his sleep, reminding him of the general nature of their business with the publishing company, and estimating the time of their return at around 7 pm. Luke finished up his simple breakfast and looked at the clock. It was still early, shortly after 9 am, so he would have to occupy himself for about 10 hours.

He strode out of the front door to breathe some fresh air and was greeted by a glorious early-summer English morning. The lawn was sparkling brilliantly, as the dew on the grass reflected the light of the sun, dispersing it in every direction. It was going to be a fair day; the sky was clear blue, and the chill was already fleeing from the morning. Luke drew a deep, refreshing breath and smiled, glad to have the day to himself, free to do as he saw fit.

Luke decided that he would spend the day exploring the surrounding countryside, but, for comfort's sake, he would wait until the dew dried to venture forth. He figured an hour or so was all that was needed to ensure that his shoes stayed dry during his explorations. He stepped back inside the cottage and decided to investigate the reading room.

The room was as he had found it yesterday, but it was lit with the early morning sunshine. The light poured in through the windows, fell across the desk, and reached its destination in the middle of the floor. The stillness in the house and the bright sunshine in the room gave Luke pause, making him wonder if the room might have looked just like this on a fine morning a hundred years ago. Luke approached the closest bookshelf and picked up a book. It was an ancient Latin tome, heavy and composed of leather pulled over boards and yellowing, but intact, vellum. Most of the books appeared of similar ilk and each looked several centuries old.

He set the book down and approached one of the maps, on the wall to the left of the desk. The map appeared to be exceedingly old, fraying at the edges and was browned by the passing of years. It seemed to be a map of England, but without any familiar landmark names that one would see on a newer one. In fact, he did not recognize *any* of the place names, and there were strange markings near where the cottage would have been located. He crossed to the map on the other side of the desk. It was an old one, to be sure, but newer than the one from which Luke had just come. It was much as he would have expected to see, with modern places and landmarks showing England as it would have been nearly a century ago. Luke was about to turn away when he noticed markings on the map in roughly the same location as the cottage would be, if placed on the map. He went back and forth several times between the two maps to ensure there was a correspondence between the markings.

Luke removed the maps from the wall, placed them carefully on the desk, and began to examine them more closely. He sat down in the wooden swivel stool in front of the desk and began poring over the maps, examining each in detail. Luke had always thought maps interesting, and these were particularly worthy of his attention. They were meticulously created and appeared to both be hand colored. The names of the locations were in a beautiful script, with stylized animals found across the maps. Given his rapt attention focused on the maps, forty-five minutes or more had passed before anything external penetrated Luke's awareness. Even then, the realization that something had changed in the room only gradually came upon him. He spun around on the stool and was startled to see a grizzled old man standing in the doorway between the reading room and the sitting room. Luke stood up quickly, unsure of the stranger in front of him.

"Don't be startled, Master Luke. I'm just the gardener. I had heard that you and your family would be here today, and I noticed you in the reading room through the window and thought I should come inside. I live in a little house just over the hill, and I walk here several days a week to tend to the gardens. I wanted to introduce myself to you," and with that, he extended his hand.

Luke returned the gesture, shaking the man's hand and sat back down on the stool, relaxing a bit with the man's introduction. The gardener had a white shock of hair underneath an old cap. He had bright, active eyes that his wrinkled skin and full-grown beard could not hide. He looked rather grandfatherly in his flannel shirt, coveralls, and well-worn work boots. His easy smile highlighted his happy disposition, and his smile widened when he noticed the object of Luke's recent study.

"It seems that you have an interest in old maps, young man. There's much to be seen in maps, especially those that you have there." He looked at the old books that Luke had put on the desk. "There's much to be seen in books too, if you know where to look."

"I was wondering what these maps were about," began Luke. "They both seem to be of the same area, but they look so different from one another. This one on the left looks older, but it doesn't look so much older that all of the locations would have different names."

The gardener smiled brightly and said, "You know, I think it'll be a hot one today, and I'm not getting any younger. Would you mind if I took the liberty of a rest and told you a story?"

"I'd love to hear one," Luke replied enthusiastically and grabbed a chair from the kitchen, allowing the old gardener a place to sit to begin his discourse. "Please, sit down. I'm sure you've earned a break," he said with a smile.

The man took his seat and removed his hat. "I'm the grandson of the man who studied in this very room," he began. "This house had been in my family for a very long time – many generations. Years ago, my family came upon hard times and had to sell the house, but I was able to strike a deal that I would be the one to care for it, which I have done for these thirty years. Enough about me, though, I want to tell you about my grandfather. He was a well-educated man, but he was a little different than most everyone else, so he never made many friends. He spent most of his time in study. It was what he studied that turned most folk off to him. He dedicated his adult life to learning about an ancient race of man-like creatures that once lived and prospered in this very land. He had only heard stories, studied legends, if you will, until one night…" He paused for a moment, as if gathering his thoughts.

"I was a little boy, probably a few years younger than you, when I first heard the story from my grandfather. It began late one night before I was born, and my father was off making his fortune miles away from here. The night was cold and blustery with a snowstorm blanketing the ground. My grandfather burst into the house, slammed the door shut behind him, and ran straight to the kitchen without even shaking himself free of snow. He grabbed a jar, stuffed some papers inside and exited the house as quickly as he had come in. A short while later, my grandfather re-entered the house, this time in a more conventional manner. He went straight to this room, but not before locking the front door and this door behind him." He turned, pointing at the door to the room in which they sat. He continued, "My grandfather was alone in the house, as my grandmother had died several years before. He had a gun with him in the reading room for self-protection. He was running from someone, but he never told who.

"The snow worked in his favor that night. He conducted his business stealthily enough, but those looking for him may have found him eventually had the blowing snow not covered his tracks almost as soon as they were made. He was never discovered but did not immediately want to take any chances. For the next several months, he lived as quietly as possible, not drawing undue attention to himself. Late that spring, I think it was around 1898, my grandfather went back into his vegetable garden and dug up a jar. In it were some of these maps that you see upon the wall, the most ancient ones. He never would tell where he got them, but evidently felt safe enough to dig them back up and begin his studies.

"Apparently, these maps show the location of a very unique place, located not too far from here. According to my grandfather's studies, this place was a site of magic and mystery and was the last holdover of an ancient race that no longer graces this earth. It is like a fading impression left by these people. This impression contains their last vestige of magic and memory. My grandfather believed that, although these people no longer existed, one could see their history, experience their magic, and feel their legacy. This place is a house, and their race is Elven." There was intensity in the old man's eyes as he said these last words, and he had been leaning forward as he told his story. He must have realized the intensity of his posture, as he sat back and softened his face.

"These maps allowed my grandfather to locate this place, although he died a disappointed man. He was convinced there was truth behind the stories but never was able to unlock the legacy left by the Elves. He didn't stop trying, though, keeping to his studies to find the key. Although he did not find it, he discovered long-forgotten stories of the Elves and their kind. My grandfather believed most of the stories to be fiction, not worth passing on, but some he was convinced had truth in them.

"He believed that they were a wondrous people, living harmoniously with their surroundings, and ruling their land with a mysterious and powerful magic. This was the land of Fay, in the time of lore. This was when legend was truth and things existed beyond current human experience. Despite their glorious beginnings, they had a rather tragic end. It seems that some of them became greedy. Some were influenced by an evil that turned them against those of their kind that were good. The Elves were their own destruction, until there was only one left. It was he who ensured their legacy, a beacon of their existence so that their race would live on in story and magic. But alas, we know but a single location and nothing else. The house my grandfather found is unique, but its story is locked. People might think me crazy, but my grandfather and I are kindred in our thoughts – I believe." The last words were almost whispered, Luke leaning in to hear, his eyes wide with wonder.

"I'm sorry to have gone on like that," the gardener apologized, abruptly breaking the tension. "It's not often I get an audience that'll listen to my rantings." He stood up and placed his hat on his head. "I had better be off. I've got some errands to run," he said with a wink.

The old man having finished his discourse, Luke found himself on the edge of his seat, intensely interested in what the man had been saying. He did not even realize his change in body posture until the man broke off his story and excused himself. Luke thanked him for the information and asked about the whereabouts of the house.

"It's over those hills," said the gardener, pointing, "toward the ocean. It's not but a few miles from here. Enjoy your day," he said with a nod and a knowing smile. And with that the gardener tipped his hat, stepped outside, and was gone.

Luke sat in the drawing room, steeped in thought about the gardener's story and the location of this mysterious house. Being that it was only late morning, Luke decided to take the walk to the house described by the old man. He grabbed a small backpack, stuffed some food and bottled water in it, and headed out for the day. Just as he stepped out of the house, however, he almost ran over a middle-aged man dressed in work clothes.

"Greetings, young man," the newcomer said with a smile. "I'm the gardener. I'll be around for a short time today tending to the gardens."

"But I was just speaking with the gardener. He was an older man, said his grandfather used to own the place," Luke replied, his eyebrows bunched in confusion.

"I'm sorry," he answered. "I'm not quite sure who you were speaking with, but there's only one gardener around here - and that's me. This house was sold to its current owner years ago, and we haven't heard of any of the previous owner's family around these parts for decades." He nodded as if the matter was settled. "I'll try to stay out of your way while I work."

"Thank you." Luke was polite but greatly puzzled. "I won't be around for a while. I'm going to do some exploring."

He pulled the door closed behind him, locked it, and headed off into the late morning sunshine, starting toward the hills indicated by the old man. It was about 45 minutes later that Luke found what he was looking for.

5

The New House

After Luke left the house, he made his way over the countryside, moving at a steady pace. He had just crested a hill about half a mile from where he started when he saw the edge of a forest on his left. It was a short way off, and it looked like it would eventually intersect with his path. He continued on, noticing a dirt road running along the forest edge. He quickly took to the road, making travel easier.

Luke was enjoying the early afternoon sunshine as he plodded along the to the summit of a small hill. There he stopped in the middle of the road to survey the pretty scene before him. He was in a little valley, created by the forest receding away to his left. A meadow sprawled out in front of him, split by the dirt road, which extended into the valley and up a larger hill. He saw a building sitting atop the hill, although he could not see it very clearly from this distance.

Luke traveled down the road into the valley, admiring the beautiful wildflowers and bright green grass swaying in the wind. The motion of the grass called his attention to the breeze, which had changed noticeably since the beginning of his walk. It had a salty smell and feel to it. He realized that he must be approaching the ocean. It was only a matter of minutes before he reached the bottom of the hill upon which the building sat. As he drew nearer, the building appeared more and more like a house. It looked to be a house of more modern construction, consisting of two storeys and finished with white siding. Although rather plain, its appearance, from his perspective, was not unpleasant. However, as Luke reached the top of the hill and swung around the front of the house, he noticed something that he had not seen before. A very short distance from the newer house stood one of much older construction. He stopped short as he gained a full view of the front of the old house.

He knew that he had seen this place before, although he could not place it immediately. He approached the house, which looked like it was centuries old, and suddenly the vague familiarity grew into an absolute certainty. This was the house from his dreams! He felt his heart jump inside of him with anticipation and excitement. Memories of the seemingly magical rooms inside filled his thoughts, and he quickly closed the distance to the ancient house to begin his exploration. As he approached the front door, he noticed a large stone anchoring the center of the archway, just as he had seen in his dreams, although without the glowing runes.

He was trembling with excitement as he reached for the iron ring hanging from the wooden door. He pushed the door open and stepped inside. Shutting the door behind him, he paused momentarily to let his eyes adjust to the relative darkness of the room. Presently, details began to emerge, and Luke was a bit disappointed to see that there was not a forest, as in his dreams. His eyes continued to adjust, however, and he noticed that it was very forest-like. Whoever had updated the interior of the house had taken great pains to create a sitting room that beautifully represented the feel of a wooded scene. Dark crown molding spread across the top of the wall and was carved into the shape of branches and leaves. Similarly, the baseboard was carved to resemble roots of great trees. In each corner of the rectangular room, a wooden corner piece ran from floor to ceiling connecting the baseboard with the crown molding, shaped like the trunk of a tree. Two-thirds of the way up the 'trunks', two beams ran at forty-five-degree angles, one on each adjacent wall, reaching up to the ceiling, carved to represent the large branches of the trees. The floor was made of flagstone and was covered in the center with a dark green rug, with a touch of brown, mimicking the moss-covered floor of a forest. Pieces of furniture, dotting the room, had been intricately crafted to represent a different element of the forest. Such was a small table that was carved to look like several intertwining saplings, supporting a glass tabletop with their carven branches and leaves. Two small windows provided some light to the room.

Although not as impressive as the room in his dreams, he was amazed at how this room looked like a forest. The details were meticulous and of the highest quality. He felt chills over his skin, as he contemplated the actual existence of this house and the similarity of this room to what he had seen in his dreams.

The furniture was arranged in such a way as to circle a fountain in the center of the room. It was built into the floor and was several feet across and about four feet high. It was made of stone, and water was bubbling from the top and spilling into the basin at the bottom. Across from the fountain, on the other side of the room, was a door. Luke walked to it knowing what he would find on the other side.

He stepped into the hallway with the four doorways represented just as he remembered. The corridor, which was about 30 feet long, had smooth, stone floors and dark wooden paneling on the walls. The only interruption to the wooden walls was the four doors and the small window at the end of the hall. He decided to enter them in the same order as in his dreams.

First entering the second door on his left, he was not surprised to find the room had a maritime theme. The floor was made of planks that could have easily come from the deck of a ship. The window opposite the door provided a view from the back of the house, opening to the ocean in the distance. Directly underneath the window was a small platform that Luke understood to represent the forecastle of a small ship. A table sat to the left of the window holding several navigational tools, such as a sextant and a spyglass, and numerous old maps of oceans and lands far and near. A ship's steering wheel was bolted to the floor on the right end of the room, and directly in the center was a post that ran from floor to ceiling, like the mast of a ship. A chair rail, crowning dark wainscoting, created the visual effect of a ship's rail going around the edge of the room. The color of the walls above the chair rail was a light blue, mimicking the sky on a clear day. The room was fascinating but far from the magical room he had seen in his dreams.

His curiosity rising to see the other rooms, Luke re-entered the hallway and went to the first door on the same side of the hall. He swung the door open and discovered a room that appeared very medieval and rounded, not unlike the inside of a castle tower. This room looked very much as he remembered it from his dream. There was a small, arched window, a blackened fireplace below a tapestry, and a rather old, ornate chest that appeared to be locked. The center of the floor was covered with a beautiful area rug that provided a soft respite from the hard stone of the floor. Next to the rug a four post-bed sat unoccupied. Finding little else in the room, he once again went out into the hallway.

Passing into the first door on the opposite side of the hallway, Luke knew to expect the least interesting room. The room was sparsely furnished. The plain walls surrounded a room that boasted only an old bed, a table, and a chair. All the furniture lacked any appreciable sign of craftsmanship or refinement and looked to be solely present to serve a purpose. Several candlesticks were found on the table, as well as some rudimentary writing implements. Curiously, the door on the opposite side that was present in his dreams was absent in this room. As plain as this room was, it was beautiful in its simplicity, and he was struck by the thought that he would like to have known the person whose room this was. He imagined the person to be humble, down to earth, and hard working. He smiled slightly at his desire to meet an imaginary person he had just created in his head.

Leaving this room, the last door in the hallway was predictably locked and provided no evidence that it could be unlocked from the outside. There were no carvings on this door, just the same bare wood he saw in his dreams. Most doors will have some give, no matter how small, when locked. This one seemed as if it was frozen in place and wouldn't budge, despite Luke's best efforts. He was fascinated by this unique house, which only served to heighten his irritation that this last door would not open.

Back outside in the sunshine, Luke had to sit down. His head was swimming. He could not believe that he had found the house that had haunted his dreams.

Not only the house, but as he looked down the hill upon which the house was perched, he marveled at the meadows, the forest, and the sea, just as in his night-time adventures. He sat there in front of the house, allowing the rhythmic pounding of the waves to calm his mind.

He knew that, somehow, he was meant to find this house. Too much had happened to him for this to be a coincidence. Although he could not yet fathom the purpose of the house in his life, he knew that he must convince his parents of its importance to him.

* * *

"Can you believe we actually bought the house?" asked Alan over a private dinner with his Catherine several weeks later.

"I'm just glad to be out of the cramped quarters of that little cottage. It was quaint, but I need to stretch my legs a bit. It is odd, though, Luke saying that he'd had a dream about the house and the need to buy it," she replied.

"I honestly don't actually know why we did it," he said with a smile. "I mean, I know we needed a house. We were going to buy one eventually, but it just seemed like we couldn't say no to Luke. He was so convinced that this was the place where we needed to be. He almost convinced *me* that this is where we're supposed to be."

Catherine chuckled a little and replied, "It seems to me that he *did* convince you of it."

"Hey, you signed the papers too," he playfully retorted. "It *is* a very interesting place, almost like two houses in one. You've got the newer one with all the modern amenities, and then you've got the other, which just seems to be a house with different themed rooms. It doesn't even have a kitchen, bathroom, or anything you would expect. It's very strange."

"The thing that gets me," she interjected, "is that no one really knows much about the older house. There was just that elderly man who claimed he built the new house so he could live next to the older one and serve as its caretaker.

35

No one really knew when the old one was built or who built it. They didn't even have a record of anyone ever owning it."

He added, "You know, there are some old buildings in this area, but parts of that one seem to be older than anything else here. Even the locals seem to act like it has always just kind of been there. Almost like it's part of the landscape or history of the area."

"Very curious."

"Indeed," he replied, starting to stand up from his seat. "Let's get home. I know we're almost done settling in, but let's get some good work done tonight. I don't want to leave Luke to do all the settling in alone."

* * *

Inside their new house, Luke was putting the final touches on his room. He was anxious to get it finished, not for the sake of having his room in order, but to free himself from the parental directive to do so.

His opportunities to revisit the old house had been extremely limited in the past several weeks and usually occurred in the company of his parents. During their short stay in the cottage, much of the family's energies were spent looking for more appropriate and permanent living arrangements. Even after the house was purchased, nearly every free minute was used moving in, unpacking, and organizing.

Luke's parents were generally fair and flexible and wanted to get his input on their final choice for housing. However, he almost didn't give them a chance to ask. After returning from his trip to the house, Luke practically accosted his parents trying to convince them to purchase 'the house on the hill'. It was like there was never really any alternative for the family, as least as far as their son was concerned.

His parents were not convinced at first and proceeded to do the obligatory house-hunting research in the local area. Although there were several attractive possibilities, things never seemed to fall into place for any of these homes. It wasn't until Luke's pestering had driven his parents to inquire about this house that the fact that there was no real owner was discovered.

To be sure, records indicated that it was private land, but there was no clear indicator of who owned it. A former resident of the newer house, claiming to be the caretaker, was declared to be the legal owner of the older building, and he was very agreeable in settling terms with Luke's family. Although Luke never met the man in the proceedings, he had a strong suspicion that this was the person he had encountered inside the cottage, who had spun such a wonderful story and virtually pointed Luke in the direction of the ancient building.

"Luke! We're back," his parents said as they entered the house. "How does your room look? Do you have it all set up?"

"It looks fine, Mom. Am I released from my indentured servitude now?" he asked with a twinkle in his eye that masked the urgency he felt.

"Oh, it hasn't been that bad, and everything's practically all set. So, I guess we can officially release you. But it's too late tonight to really do anything else. We're pretty tired, so your dad and I are off to bed, and we suggest you do the same. Get some rest, and you can do some looking around tomorrow."

Weary from several weeks of nearly non-stop work making the house livable, Luke willingly followed his mother's advice and headed back to his bedroom. Curiously, though, after an hour he found that he was having a difficult time falling asleep. His mind was preoccupied with the building next door. Although his body had been busy in the new house for the past several weeks, his mind had been dwelling on the old one. He was still baffled by its presence in his dreams and was waiting for any opportunity to explore it again. The desire to get back in the house had reached a crescendo and needed release.

A gentle breeze was blowing through his open window, ruffling the curtains, which never quite seemed to hang still. He knew that the restlessness of the curtains would only mimic his that night if he continued in bed and tried to force himself to get some sleep.

Luke quietly got up and hurriedly dressed for the night air. He opened the door to his room, crept down the stairs, and proceeded to the front door. Slipping on his shoes, he headed out of the house, closing the door noiselessly behind him. Luke knew that he could not go to sleep this night without visiting those remarkable rooms again. He could do more exploring in the morning, but he needed to see them now. Maybe it was the pale moonlight that added to the mystery of the old house and its unique rooms; something was compelling Luke to cross the threshold of the house before the night was over. Little did he know the effect venturing out that night would have on the course of his life.

6

Into the Forest

It only took a few seconds for Luke to exit his house and swing around in full view of the older building. A thrill shot through him, as he viewed the mysterious structure. His gaze was pulled to the top of the door frame, where he noticed that the markings in the stone were beginning to glow. It was just like his dream, although he now could discern the runes and know their meaning. It was an extremely odd sensation to be looking at strange markings and have them become comprehensible. He was unsure of the import of the words, as he kept repeating them in his mind, "On the other side of this door lie lands of magic, myth, and lore."

He pinched himself a few times to make sure that he was truly awake, each time receiving a painful reminder that he was. He noticed that he was getting more nervous the closer he got to the door; with each step his excitement mounted.

The sky was clear and star-filled. The moonlight was bright and seemed to cast a pale blue pallor on the stone of the house. Luke paused before the door to admire the effect of the moon on the stone, making the house strangely beautiful that night. Those thoughts of beauty lingered in his mind as he reached for the metal ring that, in his hands, would impose his will on the wooden door. As he touched the metal, energy pulsed through his body, emboldening him to push it open and step inside. He never had a chance to shut the door behind him.

* * *

Luke found himself on the edge of a forest, standing one step inside of a natural arbor that led into the trees. To his right was a large stone with markings identical to the headstone on the doorway through which he had just passed. The thought flitted through Luke's mind that this stone stood as a caution for those entering the forest. This made him pause, wondering what awaited him. Looking back for a moment, Luke saw the hill upon which his house sat, although there was no house now. He was sure that it was the same hill, and he knew it was the forest at its base that he was entering.

He took the next step and paused, tingling with anticipation, knowing that the fulfillment of his dreams was in front of him. His life had seemed so ordinary in so many ways; he was overwhelmed with the fact that what he was experiencing was actually happening to him. The dreams, the move to England, the house, and now his dreams coming true all created a surge of emotion that he had to take some deep breaths to control. Several more steps and he found himself enveloped in the forest.

The scene in front of him almost took his breath away. From the inside, the trees stood much taller than he remembered them looking from the top of the hill. There were no dead or dying trees lying around, and the forest floor was covered mostly in moss and shade flowers, most of which he did not recognize. Some of the tree trunks were massive, wider than his arms if he stretched them out. Even the smallest trees that added to the canopy were as thick as his waist. Underneath these massive trees grew smatterings of flowering trees, similar in appearance to dogwood, twenty to thirty feet in height. These trees added a splash of color to the massive height of the forest.

The ground was flat in front of him for several dozen yards before sloping gently toward a small pool of water fed by a little waterfall, not standing more than five feet tall. This waterfall was the product of a small stream that emerged from the depths of the forest. Luke moved toward the pool, scarcely able to take in the full beauty of the sylvan landscape surrounding him.

40

The last rays of the dying sun broke through the canopy, sending shafts of light that fell softly on the foliage below. This light created a dim, yet warm, atmosphere that highlighted the lush greens and the deep blue of the pool. The water ran softly, the waterfall sounding musical as it cascaded the short distance to the pool below. Green leaves slowly floated to the forest floor from the canopy above. There was just a whisper of a breeze, but not enough to explain how slowly the leaves were falling. It was as if they could barely decide between falling and being suspended in the air, deciding at the last moment to continue their downward descent. The flowering trees were also slowly dropping some petals, seemingly competing with the leaves to stay afloat. The entire effect of the ground flora and the falling leaves and petals created a forest floor that was both earthy and beautiful. There were tones of brown and green mixed in with splashes of pink and white.

On the ground sloping toward the pool, the plants grew more sparsely until directly around the water was nothing but fine sand. This soil sparkled as if it had flecks of gold and silver, surpassed only by the pure water in its shimmering effect. Some distance away, Luke could hear the songbirds singing farewell to the day and bidding the night to come forth. Their soft, high voices did not have the 'chirping' quality of any birds that he knew. Instead, these tones were steady and melodious. In fact, the more he listened, the less they sounded like actual birds. They sounded more like a choir of tiny voices hailing the serenity and wonder of their surroundings.

The sun continued to fall below the horizon, its warm glow replaced with the cool light of the rising moon. As the pool began to ripple under the magical effect of the moon's rays, Luke thought he saw something darting beneath the surface of the water. Slowly a lithe, feminine body arose in the midst of the pool, assuming the shimmer of the water and the pale blue color of the moon. Her long hair flowed behind her, and she sang in soft, liquid tones. Seemingly in response to her call, dozens of tiny balls of light dropped from the trees above, spinning and circling, continuing their song as they descended. These were not birds, after all, that sang the lovely song of the forest. As they surrounded the woman, she skipped off deeper into the woods.

Transfixed with sheer wonderment, several minutes passed before Luke dared move again. Although the woman from the water and the little spheres of light had gone, the song of the forest sang on invisibly to the lilting and swaying of the descending leaves and flower petals. Luke moved quietly to the pool wondering what other treasures it might contain. The sand was soft and noiseless underfoot, and the waterfall created a pleasant bubbling and gurgling sound, causing the water to lap up on the banks of the pool in small waves.

The water was crystal clear all the way to the bottom, and the pool was much deeper than he had expected. Although it was only about 20 feet across, it was at least that deep. It was teeming with life, small fish darting through the pool. The colors of the aquatic plants growing under the water were as vibrant as those above. Luke was amazed that he was able to see clearly to the bottom of the pool. If the water wasn't rippling on the surface, he would have wondered if he was looking through air.

As Luke studied the reflection shimmering back at him, he realized that the ambient light of the forest was not sufficient to explain the luminous water. It seemed to shine of its own accord. He stooped down, plunged his cupped hands into the water and brought them back to his mouth to drink. When the water crossed his lips, it felt pure and cool down his throat. He was instantly refreshed and seemed both invigorated and stronger at the same time. The one draught was enough; he felt no need to have more.

Having lost sight of the strange water-woman and her entourage, Luke came round to the little stream and began to follow it away from the pool. He wisely reasoned that following the water was the best course, as he had no intention of losing his way in this strange and wondrous place. The stream provided light to the forest as it wound its way along mossy banks. The soft glow was just strong enough to illuminate the surrounding trunks and touch the lower branches of the canopy. It was as if the forest provided its own night light, which softened the features of the trees, making it look almost like a beautiful painting. From time to time a leaf or flower petal would alight on the water and slowly float away on the water, reminding Luke that the stream was actually liquid and not just flowing, shimmering light.

Sometime later (Luke never knew if it was minutes or hours), a clearing appeared ahead of him, through which the stream continued on its way. He stepped into the clearing and was at once struck with the beauty of the scene. Before him stood the ruins of a once large and magnificent building. It was not a building reminiscent of those that exist now. It was made of stone but delicately constructed. Doorways were light and large, as were the windows. Decorations filled its facade, where it was still intact, incorporating patterns with no beginning or end. They were much like those of the ancient Celts, but these were more wondrous and complex. The roof had long since ceased to exist and portions of the walls had fallen in. Lush grass covered the entire area.

The ruins exuded a solemnity and peacefulness that seemed eternal. It gave one the feeling that time did not exist in this place, as if it was from an era of beauty and wonder so long ago that it almost didn't belong to this world.

There was a large break in the forest canopy over the clearing where the pale light of the moon and the bright points of the stars shone from the sky. Luke noticed the stars for the first time. They were like none that he had ever seen, sparkling like tiny diamonds bespeaking the glory of the night sky. The blackness of the firmament allowed myriads of stars to be seen, many more than in modern times, creating a depth to the universe that kept his eyes fixed on the heavens. A shooting star streaked across the sky, falling toward the horizon and bringing his eyes back to the ruins.

The stone appeared blue from the light of the celestial luminaries, while the building's surface danced with the shimmering light of the stream flowing just in front of it. Luke had never seen anything so moving in his life. He felt a lump come to his throat out of joy and reverence for this amazing place, and he resisted the temptation to fall to his knees and cry.

He walked silently toward the ruins and was approaching a break in the wall when he stopped suddenly and pulled up against the building, thinking that he heard a voice. Unsure whether it was a voice or the light breeze rustling the branches of a great tree on a warm summer night, he was about to proceed into the ruins when he heard it again. This time he felt sure it was more than just the breeze. Peering around the edge of the wall, Luke saw a human-like creature dancing on the lawn next to a beautiful blooming tree planted in the center of the ruin. Dancing it was, but dancing is a crude way of explaining what was happening. For the creature, which looked to be female, seemed to be a strange mixture of flesh and flora and appeared to almost float above the turf, moving as gracefully as branches swaying in a soft wind. Luke stood watching this solitary dance for some time before the creature slowly made her way toward the tree. There, she leaned against it, as though falling asleep, when, to Luke's amazement, she disappeared into the tree, seeming to just melt into it. A lingering impression was left with Luke that she was as much a part of the tree as its very leaves and branches.

With what he had just witnessed fresh in his mind, he did not want to disturb any part of this serene and sacred environment. So, he turned toward the stream and followed it across the clearing into the trees on the other side. This part of the forest looked very similar to what he had passed through earlier, with immense trees and smaller, flowering trees, dropping leaves and petals, which slowly descended to the ground.

The song of the forest continued on, although Luke could not see the singers. He had walked for several more minutes when the stream's character began to change. It was now flowing into a series of small pools, each lower than the other, joined in procession by a small rivulet several feet long. There were seven of these pools, not more than six or seven feet across, leading down to a larger pool at the bottom. Luke approached the lowest pool and noticed that instead of fine dirt and sand, there was stone laid around the water. The stone also formed a path leading away from the pool. As his eyes followed the path, it led to a tree of immense proportions that seemed to have flecks of silver woven into its bark. Winding its way around the trunk, a delicate staircase ascended the tree.

The evidence of an intelligent designer sent a thrill through Luke, as he longed to meet a resident of the forest. He looked back at the pools and could see now that the pools had not formed by chance. The rivulets had been carved out and, combined with the pools at differing levels, looked like a small waterfall in slow motion. The stone around the bottom pool had obviously been laid by skilled hands, as had the path to the tree.

Luke approached the sylvan giant and began to climb the stairs. Although they appeared light and delicate, they were obviously firm and strong, as they easily supported Luke's weight. In fact, the workmanship was so seamless that it appeared the stairs were part of the tree. There was no mechanism that Luke could see to indicate how the intricate staircase was affixed to the trunk as it carried him upward.

He circled his way up the tree, seemingly climbing forever. The thrill of the climb and the dizzying heights he was attaining caused adrenaline to course through his veins, sending a tingling sensation throughout his body. As he rose higher above the forest floor, the light from the stream below grew weaker, and the bottom of the canopy above appeared dark as he approached it. However, once he broke into the leaves, he found himself surrounded by thousands of points of light; the luminous voices carrying on the song of the forest were all about him, darting to and fro. They looked something like fireflies, yet these creatures were faster, their light was bluer, and he never knew fireflies to sing.

Reaching the upper branches, the winding stairway opened into a series of walkways in the branches, illuminated by the flying lights. The walkways had beautifully carved and delicate railings that would keep the traveler from falling to the forest floor below. The experience exhilarated him as he walked in the branches of these giant trees, hundreds of feet above the ground.

While exploring the forest from above, he noticed a structure that looked like a room carved into a tree at the level of the walkway. He looked down another walkway to see a similar structure in the distance. A third one appeared off to his left, reached by some pathway Luke had yet to discover. He approached the first room and saw that a walkway circumnavigated it and that a door facing him led inside. This door was beautifully carved with leaf patterns, and the handle itself was shaped like a leaf. Luke pressed on the handle, and the door slowly opened. He looked behind him, taking in the beauty of the canopy, and stepped through the door into the room. This was the last thing Luke remembered before all went black.

7

The Last of the Sonorians

Luke slowly faded back into consciousness, his head aching and his hands tied painfully behind his back. As his mind cleared and his eyes adjusted to the light, he found that he was tied to a post in the center of a room. Luke struggled against his bonds for a moment before he discovered with a start that he was not alone. His heartbeat quickened, and he ceased to struggle, discerning the outline of a figure that looked like a man. The stranger's features were hidden, backlit by a torch on the wall. All that could be seen was the man's tall, lithe build and what looked like a halo of golden hair, catching the torchlight almost as if it was shining.

"Your consciousness is to my advantage, traitor, but I daresay it is not the same for you. Where are mine enemies headed?" The voice sounded rich and full, almost melodious, but Luke did not mistake it for anything else other than deadly serious.

"I'm sorry, but I don't know what you're talking about," Luke replied in bewilderment, working subtly to free his aching hands.

"Lying does not bode well for you. Damage enough has your kind already wrought. It would be better for you if truth poured from your lips rather than blood," the stranger retorted threateningly.

"Please, sir, I don't know what you mean. I live up on the hill outside of the forest. Well… at least I did. I'm not sure where the house has gone or how I came to the forest." For the first time, Luke noticed just how hard his heart was pounding. He closed his eyes for a moment and took several deep breaths, hoping that when he opened his eyes the man would be gone. But the numbness slowly spreading in his fingers wouldn't let him forget the rope cutting off circulation to his hands.

"I do not like to repeat my words, and I am sure that you need no reminding of what I have at stake and what I might be forced to do should cooperation not be forthcoming," the stranger threatened.

Fear began to spread like wildfire in Luke, adding desperation to his words. "I *am* telling you the truth." The words began to tumble out. "Please, I don't know where I am. I don't know why I'm tied up. And I don't know who you are. I don't think that I'm supposed to be here." He paused for a moment, genuine distress weighing him down. "I really have no idea what's going on here."

"What is going on?!" the stranger roared. "What is going on?! How can you be so plainly false? Can you rightfully say that you know not of recent events? How can one in the whole of the Fay Forest and beyond know not what has commenced of late? On your life, be there no falsehood in you or it will be for the worse."

"I told you; I don't know what is going on. I don't know anything about this forest or anything that's happening." At this, Luke's voice broke, betraying the fear and confusion welling up inside him.

"This torch will allow me to better perceive the traitor before me and perhaps be used to motivate truth-telling in you," he said, as he removed the torch from the wall.

Luke almost started when the light shone on the figure's face, exposing it fully. The man, if you could call him that, was extraordinary. His eyes were large and bright, being the color of the full moon on a clear, dark night. They seemed to see right through Luke. There was a deadly seriousness in them, but they did not appear cruel. His skin was pale, but the paleness did not indicate weakness; the strength of steel was seen in his flawless face. In fact, most would think him beautiful. His long hair was pulled back behind his head and was a rich yellow, having the reflective sheen of metal. He wore a thin sort of crown that was made of gold, indicating a prominent position among his people. Rich green and brown robes encompassed him, accented by golden flecks and swirls in intricate and endless patterns. There was no hair upon his chin, making him look almost boyish. However, no one would make the mistake of calling him a boy. In fact, Luke was not sure that he had seen anyone look so masculine before in his life. The tops of his ears were drawn to a point and were angled toward the back of his head. Now, Luke had read many legends in his life, and if his distress had not so clouded his thinking, he would strongly suspect that he was in the presence of an elf - but not like the elves of modern stories. This one was both terrifying and captivating, the stories capturing only a cheap caricature of the real thing. What startled Luke most about this person was not the obvious strangeness of his mien, but the presence of seemingly contradictory elements at the same time. He was both beautiful and fierce, strong yet elegant, boyish yet manly. His captor was instantly unlike anyone Luke had ever seen before.

"Please sir, I see that you're desperate, but you're not cruel. I can see that in you. I don't know who you are or how I got here. Please let me go," pleaded Luke.

His captor paused and took a long look at Luke under the light of the torch. "Now I am upon you close I see there is a telling difference in your face from those of mine enemies." His hard features softened somewhat, and his muscles relaxed. "Your eyes hold no guile, and hatred is not stamped on you. Suspicion has become my only friend as of late, so forgive me if caution is paid its due before freedom is yours. Now before I release you from your bonds, tell me how it is that you happened upon this place."

Luke began with his story of his strange dreams, the discovery of the house, and the stone at the entrance to the forest that seemed to be identical to the one in the doorway of the house. He struggled a bit in the telling, as he knew much of his life would only be confusing to his captor. Upon the completion of his narrative, he was reasonably satisfied that he had conveyed the important points without delving much into his modern world.

After Luke had finished, his captor concluded, "'Tis a strange tale you bear. I only know of one such stone, but it was made of strange magic generations ago to protect the forest. I know not of any house upon the hill. Truly, I have not ventured far out of the forest, as it is my home and is the kingdom of my people." At this, his face fell, and he corrected himself. "It *was* the kingdom of my people. We are dying, and with our passing so does the protection and enchantment of the forest."

Luke wondered at his words, "I can't believe the strange things I've seen tonight. How could the enchantment be dying?"

"Before I burden you with my sad tale, let me first untie you, friend. I see that there is no danger with you. Friends are rare in this age, and I would not deny my last one hospitality this night."

He began, "My people are an ancient race, and magical. We have lived in harmony with this forest since time unremembered and have relied on it for life. Likewise, the forest has relied on us. We call it the Fay Forest, and its beauty and enchantment are sustained by my people. We are the lifeblood of the forest. In turn, the forest has allowed us to rule it with gentleness and peace for many years. However, this has all changed and much to our calamity.

"In my lifetime, the my people had a terrible disagreement. A faction of my people wanted to exploit the forest and expand our rule beyond the borders, conquering other realms. The other side did not, for peace was too valuable, and we had no need for conquering; Paradise had been granted to us. Although we continued to co-exist, our race was divided. The Malicians, for so we called them, desired only domination and that through malice, while the Sonorians, those who stayed true, valued peace and harmony. The Malicians were thought to be too weak to be a serious threat outside the Forest, and we tolerated them. That was the gravest mistake in the annals of our history.

"There are creatures that exist beyond the Forest. We knew this before, but perhaps our peaceful ways had blinded us. Peace was our way, but we have learned it is not the way of all things. While peace was proffered to us in falsehood, the Malicians ventured from the Forest. What they brought back was a force more destructive than any in the Forest had ever seen. With them came a race of beings driven by greed and war. They are called Hyu-mans.

They are sweeping through the Forest destroying all traces of the Sonorians. The resemblance you bear to them is what so aroused my suspicion." He paused for a moment before summoning a sad smile. "My name is Ayne, and I am the last of the Sonorians."

"How can you be the last? What's happened to them all?" asked Luke in surprise.

"All have been killed. Evil overtook the Malicians, twisting their intentions; they have been poisoned by the Hyu-mans and will be turned upon next, though they know it not. The beauty and enchantment of the Fay Forest is sustained by the life force of my people. The Spirit of the Trees, the Spirit of the Waters, and the Lights of the Forest will all be gone. They will die with me, the last Sonorian."

"How have you managed to survive?" Luke interjected.

"I was the leader of the last of the Sonorians, there were none else. We had resisted the Hyu-mans as well as we could and were searching for a place of safety. Alas, my wife, stopping for a rest, was separated from the group. I perceived her absence and struck out to find her just before the trap was sprung. We were ambushed, and our families slaughtered. While I did not see my family slaughtered, as did the rest of my kin before their demise, I never found my wife. Grief consumed me. I was nearly driven mad before regaining my senses after many days. I eluded pursuit and have been wandering the ancient forests of my ancestors without purpose other than survival. I am the last. There are none to follow. The next generation died with my wife. All hope will die with me."

"What will you do now?" wondered Luke aloud.

"I know not what the future holds for me. As the last of my kind, I can save nothing but myself, and that is the bane of my existence. I dare not give myself up, for if I do, the sun will have set on us forever. The enchantment will be gone. If I dedicate myself to life, I will only be prolonging what I cannot forever escape. A solitary existence is my fate, eluding my pursuers until I can no longer. This ring I bear will be the last reminder of a great people. It will soon be lost to time as my body returns to the forest, as all who have come before me."

Ayne held forth his hand, the ring glinting in the moonlight. It was shining white gold inlaid with yellow gold, tracing intricate threads across the surface. There were two yellow strands that gracefully crisscrossed the ring, giving it a stunning and elegant appearance.

"There has got to be something that can be done. What about the Malicians? There must be some good ones left that can preserve your line," Luke suggested.

"The Malicians are dying also. Although they know it not, I have seen it. I have seen scores of Malicians being led to the slaughter at the hands of the Hyu-mans. Hyu-mans have twisted them to their own purposes, used them to kill their own kind, and are now exterminating them, although they hide this from the remaining few. The Malicians are blind in their ignorance, and my life is forfeit if I return to them. I wait for hope no longer. But you, you are different than I. You come from another land. You may still cling to hope." He paused for a moment before continuing, as if returning to the present. "My fear is that we have tarried long enough in this place. I would not expose you to peril needlessly. Arise. Let us remove ourselves to a place less conspicuous than this. The forest represents danger to us. Its beauty is waning, and its protection can no longer be relied upon. Should ill fortune find us, make for the valley out of which you came."

Ayne pulled Luke to his feet, led him through the door and out into the walkways among the treetops. It was still night with bright points of starlight filtering through the forest canopy. In the east, however, the first touches of morning were blessing the sky. Luke wondered that such a serene and beautiful place could be under the power of such evil and destruction.

Luke did not know where he was being led, but he made sure that he kept pace with Ayne, who moved with a sense of compelling urgency. They progressed quickly, moving in a northerly direction, back toward the valley that had brought Luke into the forest the night before.

Ayne led Luke along the treetop pathways to a massive tree and down a winding staircase that led them back to the forest floor. Their flight left no time to appreciate the grandeur around them, and the magic of the night before seemed all but gone in the early light of morning. In fact, Luke's wondrous experience from the night before seemed a distant memory in the face of the hidden threat from which they ran.

No sooner had Luke's foot touched the ground than the twang of a bow sent an arrow flying between them, sticking fast in the trunk of the tree. More quickly than Luke could have imagined, Ayne was off through the forest, pulling Luke after him. He moved with incredible speed, so much so that Luke was inevitably falling behind.

Looking back, Ayne slowed and yelled to Luke, "My life is what they seek. You have no part in this business. Turn aside and hide, then head to the valley."

"I can't just leave you to die," Luke panted. "Come with me into the valley if it's safer."

"Safer it may be for you; the forest is my only companion now. As long as I exist, the forest can offer me more protection than the woodless places. Our ways must part here, friend."

"There has to be something I can do," Luke protested breathlessly.

"There is. You must leave. I cannot have your life on my conscience. You are no party to my problems. Depart from me. You cannot match my swiftness. I will lead them away from you."

"But I'm not sure that I know how to get to the valley," Luke said, suddenly fearful as the realization came to him. Ayne then realized that his course was set. He must lead Luke into the valley and depart from the protection that the forest afforded him.

While they had slowed to plot their course, the sounds of the active pursuit of their enemies came crashing through the forest.

"Follow me," were the only words Ayne spoke as he raced toward the valley.

It was not long before the trees began to spread out, allowing more and more sunlight through the thinning canopy, signaling the edge of the forest. However, the pursuit of the enemy was closer and closer, as Ayne had to temper his speed to keep Luke near. In a last mad dash, the two fleeing figures spilled out from the forest into the bright sunlight of morning with their pursuers just behind.

8

Battling Unbelief

Luke picked himself up from the dewy grass and took off at a full sprint. In an instant, he knew something had changed. The previous moment he had been in the bright morning sunshine, and now he was blanketed by night. He slowed down and cautiously looked around. The stars were his only pursuers. He did not find himself at the cusp of a forest, rather he was now standing at the top of a hill with only his ragged breaths punctuating the night silence. Spinning around, he looked squarely at his home.

He was back home and thoroughly confused. Following his footprints in the dew, he made his way back to the older house and found a portion of tussled grass where he had lain momentarily after leaping through the door. The door was still open, and he stepped cautiously back inside. He found the room as he had first seen it when he explored the house in the daylight. It was a unique room, to be sure, but there was no hint of magic in it. He went back outside to look at what had been the glowing capstone above the front door, and it was as dark and cold as any ordinary stone that might be in its place.

Luke began to wonder if the whole experience had been a dream. But he could not fully explain the fact that he had been out of his bedroom and running around in the dew of the pre-dawn morning. He also could not adequately explain the seeming reality of what he had just experienced. It appeared every bit as real as what he was encountering now.

Despite the incredible experience he just had, the only reasonable explanation was that he had, for some reason, been sleepwalking and had a dream related to the room. The house had so captured his imagination that it must have created a super-realistic dream. As the other dreams about this house came flooding back into his memory, this explanation became more convincing. During his short walk back to his house and into his bedroom, he had just about convinced himself that his nocturnal adventure had been but a dream.

* * *

The sun shining through Luke's bedroom window ushered him into the morning. He felt surprisingly well rested, despite his sleepwalking adventure from last night. As the stars gave way to the sun, the seeming reality of the night before again gave way to the need to have a reasonable explanation for his experience. Despite wanting to believe what had happened to him was real, Luke succeeded in all but banishing any possibility that it was anything other than a dream.

However far from reality he might push the night before, he was plagued all the following day by remembrances of his time in the Fay Forest and the plight of Ayne and his people. He allowed himself to acknowledge that he had never had a dream that was quite so vivid or affected him as much as this one did. In fact, there wasn't much else he thought about the following day, or days thereafter for the next several weeks.

His parents noticed Luke's preoccupation and were worried that he was struggling with his transition to his new home. His frequent assurances didn't completely dislodge this concern, although they decided that their repetitive questions wouldn't help him open up to them.

Alan was rather busy with his new job and was beginning to travel across England and Scotland visiting different office locations. Wanting to expose Luke to as much of the United Kingdom as possible and hopefully get him to relax and open up, he took his family with him on these occasions.

Luke thoroughly enjoyed his travels with his parents, visiting such places as Cornwall, Kent, London, Sherwood Forest, and Edinburgh. He saw much of the beauty of the country and many ruined reminders of medieval glories past. He learned about the history of the island, of the pagan Celts, of the Anglo-Saxons, and their conquerors, the Normans. He visited Tintagel Castle and many other locations of myth and legend, among them those associated with King Arthur himself. However, none of these travels, as enjoyable as they were, could divert his mind for long from his night in the old house. He thought about it often during these days. And though his dreams escaped him at night, he was somewhat comforted by the absence of further sleepwalking episodes while he was traveling with his family.

Finally, toward the end of the trip, he decided to talk to his parents about his dream in the hopes that talking about it would decrease the compulsion to think about it. After several awkward tries, he addressed his parents at breakfast one morning, "Mom and Dad, I want to talk to you about something. It's not that big of a deal, but I just want to talk to someone about it."

"Sure, Luke, what is it?" asked Alan.

"Well, about two weeks ago, shortly before we left on this trip, I think I was sleepwalking one night. I found myself outside of the old house."

"Were you okay?" Concern filled his mother's voice, "Did you get hurt?"

"No, I didn't get hurt. It was just strange, that's all. Do people just start sleepwalking? Can it happen only once?"

Alan replied, "I don't know that much about sleepwalking, but I'm sure that there are lots of people out there that do it just once or twice. You might want to lock your door at night or something, just to make it a little harder for you to get out of your bedroom. We don't want to take any chances of you getting hurt."

"I understand. I obviously don't want to get hurt either, although that's not my biggest concern. I had the strangest dream about a different land corresponding to the front room of the house. It's like I stepped through the door, and I was someplace else. It's too much to explain now, but when it was all over, I found myself back outside the front door. That's when I realized I had been sleepwalking."

"Well, it is a strange house, and very curiously decorated. I'm sure that its uniqueness was just playing on your imagination and found itself in your dreams. I'm not sure how it's related to the sleepwalking, but just be careful from now on," Alan concluded.

"Yes, do be careful. I think locking the door at night might be a good idea. Whatever you decide to do, let us know if it happens again. I wonder if this has to do with the upheaval in your life since the move…"

Luke tuned out the rest of what his mother was saying, he had heard it enough from her. He was being pulled back into his thoughts. The conversation had not gone like he had hoped, although he wasn't sure how he would have wanted it to go. He just knew that they didn't seem to grasp how this dream had affected him, and he wasn't sure how to relay it to them. It felt like it would take too much work to explain everything, but they couldn't understand, as they hadn't shared the experience with him. The result was that Luke was somewhat ashamed for having told them, and his thoughts about the Fay Forest had not abated for having done so.

The rest of the trip generally went well, and Luke resolved to not be conquered by his thoughts. He enjoyed his trip as much as he could, but not nearly so much as he had hoped, or would have had the trip taken place before his dream. The truth be told, Luke was looking forward to getting back to the house, to enter again at night to see what would happen. Although he would not admit it to himself at the time, part of Luke wanted to believe that it was not a dream. This emotional part was small and daily defeated by his reason. The defeat was not total, however, and Luke found himself deciding to go back to the house the first night upon his return.

Unfortunately for Luke, he and his family arrived back home early in the morning after traveling all night. He was bleary-eyed and tired and slept into the early afternoon. His parents were home that day, and Luke did not want to make obvious his plans to get back into the old house.

Having time in the afternoon and evening, Luke pondered once again the experience that he had. His heart wanted to believe that it was real. Between his dreams, the house, and his recent experience, there were too many odd coincidences for it just to have been a dream. The thought that something inexplicable was happening in his life gave him a thrill of excitement. This was quickly chased away, however, by a fear of the unknown. Why was it happening to him? Was he being chosen, or was this all an accident? The implications of these questions caused a shudder to pass through him, making self-distraction his priority for the rest of the evening.

He wasn't content sitting quietly in his room waiting for the hours to pass. He tried to burn off the energy by walking the grounds, only to find himself constantly drawn to the old house. This didn't help to distract him, so he decided to head to the village to spend the afternoon.

The village square was quaint and contained a pub, a florist, a small antique store, and a corner store that sold some groceries, among other buildings scattered across the village center. The buildings were clearly several centuries old and were constructed of a soft gray stone and had slate roofs. There was a stone cross on a green across from the pub to which Luke gravitated.

He sat down on a bench and watched the people going about their business. This served to distract him only for a short time before his mind began to wander back to his plans for the evening. He realized that he needed a more active distraction than people-watching, so he got up and decided to peruse the antique shop, which was on the opposite side of the green from the pub. Luke found a fair selection of old books in the store, which, being a book lover, finally succeeded in occupying his mind.

Slowly, the heat of the day began to abate, as the golden orb sank toward the horizon. The light was fading when Luke arrived back home, and the plans for the evening came crowding back into his mind. He became nervous just thinking about revisiting the house. But it was a nervousness blanketed in excitement, and he was trembling with the expectation of going back into the house. The effort that he had put into denying the reality of his experiences was not enough to temper the visceral anticipation that he was feeling.

Despite his doubt, he realized that if something did happen, he should be better prepared this time. He picked up a backpack and packed some extra clothes and a jacket, just to make sure that he would be warm. A pocketknife was thrown in, as was a compass, a flashlight, gloves, and a warm hat. Proceeding downstairs to the pantry, he also grabbed some food items and poured himself a thermos of water. As inconspicuously as possible he went back up the stairs to his bedroom, determined to wait until his parents went to bed before he stole out into the night.

Although Luke pretended to be busy, fiddling around with books and papers at his small desk, his focus eluded him. He went to lie down on his bed and think through his plan for the evening again. Being on his feet all day and working to suppress his nervous energy must have tired him more than he had anticipated. Before he knew what was happening, the weight of fatigue had fallen on him, transporting him into sleep.

What must have been hours later, Luke snapped into consciousness wondering what time it was. Angry at himself for falling asleep, he was afraid that his opportunity had passed. He turned the clock toward him; it was just past 2:30 am. There was still time to act, but he was cursing himself as he silently slipped down the stairs toward the front door. He paused to shake the sleep from his head and try to calm the butterflies that fluttered in his stomach. Gripping the doorknob and turning it slowly, he took care to avoid making any noise. As he stepped across the threshold, he shut the door silently behind him.

The moon broadcast its pale light through the atmosphere, and it lit Luke's slow steps to the old house. He could feel his feet dampen from the dew as he crossed the short distance between his front door and the house that had dominated his thoughts for most of his waking hours. His fingers tingled with anticipation as he approached it, his heart pounding within his chest. The night held a slight chill, yet there were small beads of sweat forming on his forehead. Not knowing what he would find caused him to feel a stab of fear, but he knew what he needed to do. He must know for sure if this house was truly enchanted or if it was all just a dream.

His pace quickened as he approached the door. He reached out for the metal ring and opened it. Luke steadied himself with a deep breath and plunged into the darkness of the house to see where it would take him.

9

The Gael

Luke slowly exhaled and opened his eyes. He could see nothing but darkness. He found his flashlight and turned it on. Disappointment flooded his face. It was as he had found it before - very interesting, but still just a room. From somewhere deep inside, he almost felt like crying. Part of him had wanted to go back, back to the enchantment, to the Fay Forest, to help Ayne and his cause. The realization that it was a dream was almost too much for Luke. The room seemed less enchanted to him than ever before, but much more meaningful. Even if his time with Ayne wasn't real, this room would forever remind him of his dream in that magical place.

Luke was tempted to turn and walk out of the house and return to his bed. Something changed his mind, though. Maybe it was nostalgia for the first time that he had laid eyes on the house in his dreams. Thinking back, he remembered the awe that he felt as this very room seemed a veritable forest within the house. He then remembered moving through the room into the hallway, watching himself in his mind's eye enter the last room on the left, which resembled a ship. What an adventure it would be if that room was more than just a room. Luke loved the sea and harbored romantic notions of adventures and pirates. Maybe he had read Robert Louis Stephenson too many times, but the urge to see the room again became almost overwhelming. It had, in fact, been a while since he was able to spend any time in the house, and since he was out of bed, he might as well make good use of it.

With the flashlight pointed at the door in the back of the room, he slowly proceeded toward the hallway. Reaching the door, he opened it in a slow and solemn manner, peering around it before proceeding through. Once again, nothing seemed unusual, and a pang of disappointment struck him for the second time that night.

What could I really expect to be here? he thought. *It's not real. I don't know why I keep hoping.*

But hope pulled Luke down the hallway, closer to the last door on the left. He stood gazing at the amazing handiwork carved on the front of the door. Old romantic notions of the sea flooded into his mind. It was as if the door awakened something buried deep within him. A sense of adventure, determination, and purpose struck Luke forcefully. He grasped the handle and said a short prayer of hope. He swung open the door and stepped through.

Luke was thrown from his feet. His flashlight flew from his hands, as he rolled on the floor of the room. He was wholly unprepared for what was happening to him. Despite being thrown, Luke was able to keep a steady head and noticed that there were a good many other things amiss in the room. It was dark. But Luke, his eyes adapted from trudging around at night, noticed thousands of stars staring at him from above. It was still night, wherever he was. Where silence should have been, it was replaced with the melodious sounds of water lapping up against something. He got to his feet, grabbed his flashlight, and scrambled to the nearest solid object that he could find. Taking hold of a small mast, he steadied himself to look around. It took a few seconds for him to come to the full realization that he was actually on a ship.

Although no expert, Luke knew a few things about seafaring vessels, and decided that he was on something very similar to a caravel. Compared to a military or trading vessel, it might have appeared small, but it was a handsome ship used for private purposes.

The sea was calm enough for Luke to gain his footing quickly and explore the decks of the ship. He saw a small, raised deck in front of him, serving as the forecastle. Behind him was a rather large and higher deck, presumably under which was the captain's quarters. A waist-high rail ran around the entire ship. There was only a light wind, and the sails were furled. The ship was moving forward, it appeared, but very slowly, mainly by the workings of the sea.

Luke quit his post at the aft mast and carefully proceeded to the foremast. For the first time, his surroundings really began to sink in. He smelled the salt air and listened to the gentle noises of the waves. The sea breeze ruffled his hair and exhilarated him. As the stars twinkled down upon him from their heavenly perch, a sense of peace and comfort stole upon him. He breathed the air and breathed strength. He listened to the water and heard music. He looked at the stars and saw wisdom. These stars were the same that were gazed upon by the ancients and have seen all the endeavors of mankind.

The celestial majesty had stolen Luke's attention. Stars had always been a constant source of wonder for him. They represented something bigger and more beautiful than he could imagine, and tonight they seemed to be calling to him, calling him to a purpose larger than himself. Luke closed his eyes to drink in the pleasure of his surroundings, to feel the breeze caressing his face, and to listen to the language of the sea.

In Luke's tranquil state, he started when he heard the words, "I would not move if you value your life." He opened his eyes to find the source of the voice. Standing not five feet away was a man of a strong but slender build pointing a sword in his direction.

"Who are you and what manner of business have you aboard the *Gael*?"

"I'm sorry sir. I don't really know how I came aboard. I was in a house and opened a door, and I found myself on this ship. I don't mean any harm," stated Luke shakily.

"Through a door, you say. How comes one from a house to a ship through a door? No such door have I seen that possesses such qualities," said the captain.

"Well, I don't know about the door, except that it was in a house that seems to be magical. This is not the first place that it's taken me. I mean you no harm, and I don't know where I am," offered Luke.

The stranger appeared interested but did not drop his sword. "Gained you access to this other place through the same door?"

"No," replied Luke. "It was a different door. There are five doors in the house. The one that brought me here was carved with images of the sea. It made me long so much for the sea that I could barely help but to step through."

"I have an interest in these doors of which you speak. I have heard of some such portals. Legend says that they were created from trees grown in forests lost with time, trees of a different quality than we find now. It has been years since I thought upon these stories. Your tales may be interesting, but discernment is prudent in the presence of strangers. Lay down your possessions and move on top of the forecastle."

Luke complied, setting down his backpack and flashlight and climbing the several stairs to mount the deck in the front of the ship. He watched as the captain cautiously approached his backpack and emptied its contents. All of his things lay on the deck of the ship, the captain picking through them, searching for any hidden weapons. Most of them he viewed as innocuous but took a fascination with the flashlight. He pressed the button and was startled by the beam of light that came forth.

"What manner of magic is this?" asked the captain.

Many thoughts rushed through Luke's head as he thought how he might explain the concept of a flashlight to this individual. "It's not magic at all, sir. I don't really know how it works either, but where I'm from some very smart people have found a way to store energy and turn it into light. Beyond that, I don't know how to explain it. It is through science, not magic that the light is made."

"I do not know how to respond to this, and if you do not even know its workings, my questions will remain unanswered. What is it that you call this?" queried the stranger.

"It is called a flashlight, and you can keep it as a gift. Use it to see things better at night, but do not leave the light on for long, as the saved energy will last only a short time and will be all used up." Presenting the flashlight as a token of friendship, Luke's mind returned to his predicament. "Sir, I am not armed. I don't know how I got on this ship, and I don't know who you are. You don't have to keep me on board any longer than you want to, but I don't know where I am or what I'd do."

"You have a trustworthy look about you," said the captain, "and I believe that I can judge character rightly, so I will keep you aboard for the time being. I accept your gift, and I will return your pack to you. Be forewarned; I will be observing you closely. I am no fool, and will not be had by trickery, should I have misjudged you."

Luke felt greatly relieved at this and introduced himself, "I am Luke, and I'm glad to meet you." Luke extended his hand in greeting. The man mounted the forecastle and did the same. A firm but friendly grip closed around Luke's hand.

"My name is Declan. I am a lord in England, and I sail under the protection of the King."

* * *

Luke slept on an empty cot in the very front of the forecastle, somewhat separated from the half-dozen or so crew also sleeping there. They had been awakened and informed of Luke's presence and that he was to be allowed to sleep undisturbed. He slept through what remained of the night and through most of the next day. It was late in the evening when Luke went back above deck. There he found Declan alone on the forecastle watching the sun set. Luke slowly approached him.

"Luke…," Declan mused. "It is a strong name." He uttered those words in acknowledgment of Luke's arrival but without turning to greet him.

Luke remained silent and came abreast to Declan, gazing at the streaks of yellow, orange, and red that graced the sky. He thought he had never seen such a sunset, as if an artist had chosen the richest hues of the palate and splashed them across the sky. The undulating water reflected the light and made the oncoming night appear so much the richer.

"Had sleep not ruled your day, my family would like to have met you. Stowaways excite the imagination of my children."

"Sir, with all due respect, I am not a stowaway," Luke protested. "I just entered through a door and found myself here…"

"Tell me Luke," Declan interrupted, "what would you suggest I tell my family? I think it best that we portray you as a friendly stowaway, brought to our boat by some fortunate accident."

"I understand," Luke acknowledged and then fell silent.

Declan returned the silence as both stood drinking in the heavens. The strangeness of the situation crept upon Luke. He was standing abreast with a nobleman on his ship, riding the high seas, taking in the most beautiful sunset he had yet witnessed in his young life.

Declan turned toward Luke slightly as the sun sank lower into the sea. His brow knitted and his face seemed thoughtful. "Last night I was troubled in my sleep. There is something different about you. I know not whether that bodes good or ill, but there is a prescience to my thoughts that this was meant to be. I believe that higher powers than we know have determined this meeting." His face lightened, "But let there be some familiarity amidst mystery. You know my name and naught else."

Declan spun around and pointed to the mast. "I fly under my family's crest. The higher flag represents my family, and the lower represents the protection afforded by the king. As long as the king's flag flies, we shall sail peacefully."

The uppermost flag piqued Luke's interest, as it was a brilliant field of blue and contained a crest of gold, accented by a stunning red rose. Luke could see the flags snapping in the salty wind, lit by the crimson rays of the departing sun. Behind the flags, the stars were beginning to emerge from the black void that the sun was leaving behind.

Declan, noticing the stars, pointed to an especially bright one and said, "Do you see that bright star? It is the brightest you will see this even'. There are three stars to the south, trailing from it. The second star from the bottom is flanked on either side by stars. Those six stars are the most precious to me in all the heavens. They are The Sword of Ayne the Last."

Luke's heart jumped in his chest, and he often wondered whether it jumped first at the mention of Ayne or at the sight of the ring on Declan's finger, highlighted by the last ray of the sun before it succumbed to the night. He was almost sure that it was identical to the one shown him by Ayne in his previous adventure.

"Legend has it," Declan continued, "that this land was once peopled by creatures different than man. I say different, but I mean better. They were holy. They were lovely. They were good. They could bring the earth to life. Forests were alive; the trees swayed, and the water ran. Not like we've seen them do it. They moved of their own volition. There was an enchantment that ruled, that ran through everything, that gave it life and love and mirth. It is said that the enchantment and the people in whom it lived were betrayed, betrayed by their own. The betrayal was total, and all was lost, save one. It is said that one of the true Elves made it through, Ayne. He was the last, or so the legend goes. I have known that story since I was a child, and I love to tell it. But what I love the most is what I now tell you, and it is not of legend. I believe that it is of truth. It does not linger on the lips of the common people, but in the hidden vales of the country. It is whispered in the tops of the oldest forests. It is breathed in the wooded streams. There, if you listen carefully to the ancient story told by the land itself, you will hear, fainter and fainter as the years pass, that Ayne had a descendant. The question that I pose, and have wondered for my whole life, is how could he have a descendant if he was the last?"

Luke saw a curious twinkle in the eye of the captain as the last words came forth. Declan left the prow of the ship and headed toward the cabin. He paused at his door and spoke softly to Luke, "May your sleep be peaceful. I will see you on the morrow."

Luke was left on the prow alone with his thoughts, the starlit, moonless sky, and the ceiling of clouds that had slowly appeared from the west. The wind had picked up and Luke found the night somewhat chilly. He descended below to see what sleep the night would give him so he could serve a purpose the next day. He was also eager to meet the family of this interesting nobleman.

10

The Gale

Luke awoke in confusion. The world seemed to be crashing down around him. He heard yelling but could not discern its location, due to the crashing noise of the ocean and the wind. It was completely black in the forecastle, and Luke found himself alone. He crawled out of his bed to see what was going on when a deafening crack overtook all the other noise around him. Although the sound lasted only seconds, it shook the air, which seemed to be momentarily tinged with power, a current that made his hair stand on end. The ship lurched to starboard with a crash, and Luke was thrown from his feet, barely missing a rafter with his head. He regained his footing and found the ladder leading to the topside. Bracing himself against it as the ship lurched again, he began climbing. He opened the hatch only to have it promptly snatched from his hands by the wind, slamming back against the deck. Chaos and confusion greeted him, accompanied with stinging rain and heavy winds.

The night was thick and without stars. The clouds formed in the west held sway and stirred up what had been peaceful waters. Huge swells washed over the ship, sweeping overboard anything that was not tied down. A brilliant bolt of lightning stretched across the clouds in the sky directly above them, illuminating the source of the deafening noise just moments earlier. Lightning had struck the mast, snapping if off near the base. Luke watched in horror as it crashing over the side of the ship.

Shuddering at the whipping wind and rain, Luke was momentarily unsure of his next move. Surprisingly, he thought not of the danger he would assume by climbing on to the deck of the storm-tossed ship. Rather, he thought of the agony of passing the night alone in the forecastle, being tossed from wall to wall not knowing how the men were faring above, just waiting helplessly for whatever fate would claim him.

He slid onto the deck and looked for the closest thing to grab. Fortunately, there was a secured cargo net near him, and Luke grasped it for dear life. There were men all around him, working the ship, securing cargo and sails, and trying to assess the damage caused by the falling mast, all while doing their best not to be washed overboard.

Declan was aft yelling orders, most of which were drowned out by the wind and the rain. Lightning flashed again, and its partner thundered afterward. The sky lit up in the distance behind him, highlighting his strong form grasping the wheel, trying to keep the ship's course, despite the efforts of the violent sea. Suddenly, a pulley attached to a rope came loose and swung toward Declan. This Luke saw in the split second it took for the aura of the lightning to die away. He released his grip on the cargo net and struggled toward Declan. He was able to reach the staircase to the aft deck just as the ship tossed again. Luke slammed into the railing, almost spilling over it and into the ocean. Quickly regaining his composure, he climbed the now precarious stairway onto the deck, spied the wheel and found it unmanned, spinning in the wind. Luke's heart jumped in his chest just before discerning a heap against the starboard rail. The lurching ship tossed Luke down, and the slippery deck and the wind made it nearly impossible to regain his footing. What seemed like many minutes was mere seconds before he was able to slide over to Declan, who lay injured and unconscious.

Luke yelled for help, hearing his words die in the wind almost as soon as they were uttered. The men were working on the deck below, and there were none close enough whose attention Luke could arrest. He steadied his position with his right hand on the rail and his left arm around Declan's shoulders. Luke knew that none could hear him in the din of the storm, and even his own life might be forfeit if he did not act quickly. He put both arms around Declan and pushed off the rail with his feet, aiming at the stairs up which he had climbed.

His had almost made it, when the ship was hit by a massive wave on its prow. This thrusted the prow into the air, throwing Luke head over heels from his unsecured position, causing him to lose his grip on Declan. He was thrown into the rail at the back of the top deck, and Declan had dropped to the deck and was sliding down toward Luke. Just as soon as the ship had lifted, the prow ducked down into the trough that followed the wave. Better prepared this time, he moved toward Declan, grabbing him as he slid past. He reached and caught hold of the stair rail and held as fast as he could.

Luke was able to start down the stairs when a deckhand noticed his plight and came to assist and, between the two of them, were able to get Declan below into the forecastle to be tended. Luke was the obvious choice for this job, as he had no sailing experience. Once down below, the hatch was closed, and Luke hoisted Declan's large, limp frame into a sailor's bed. The remainder of the dark and violent night was spent in the even darker front cabin, making sure that no further injury awaited Declan as the ship tossed like a toy boat in a raging river.

* * *

Morning's light brought calmer seas and consciousness to Declan. The threat of further danger now passed, some of the sailors came down to check on their captain and report the safety of his family. Several lanterns were lit to discover the extent of his injuries. Sitting on the edge of the cot with a pounding headache, he winced as a ship-hand gingerly touched the large bump on the back of his head. "Must you touch it?! I do not wish to be intimates with pain whilst on this trip."

"I didn't mean no 'arm, sir. Just waren't sure if you was bleedin'," the man muttered, in a thick, Cockney accent.

"I know. No harm done, just help me to my feet." As he said this, he stood and almost toppled over, feeling a rush of lightheadedness overtake him.

Luke and several of the men leapt to their feet to stabilize the captain and help him recover. Once steadied, he made his way to the ladder, mustered his strength and climbed out onto the deck. The blazing sun of the morning hurt his eyes, and he stood atop the ladder for a few moments, shielding his face as he got used to the light. The gently rolling deck was a sharp contrast to the violence of the ship during the night before.

"Sir, 'e saved yo' life an' tended to ya' all the night long," stated the shipmate who had helped Luke and Declan below deck the night before. "I didn't know 'e 'ad made it above an' thar 'e was up yonder with you in tow, sir."

"Is this true?" asked Declan. "It appears that I owe more to you now than just my hospitality. It must have been providence that brought you on board. Many thanks and God's blessings to you on this fortuitous occasion. You have saved my life."

"Sir, if you are the type of man you seem to be, I could have done no less," said Luke, meaning every word.

"I hope to settle this debt someday, but for the present I must survey the damage to the *Gael* and discern whether safe harbor needs be attained for repairs," and he swung round to inspect the stump that remained of the main mast. Jagged wood and splinters signaled the absence of the support for the ship's mainsail. There was damage on the side rail where the mast had fallen. Fortunately, the structure of the ship remained largely unharmed, as the mast seemed to have crashed through the rail and flipped into the sea. The ship was not leaking, and the deck appeared intact. However, the missing mast and mainsail presented a problem. The men were complaining about the lack of speed and the difficulty of replacing what had been lost, while Declan considered a potentially more problematic and dangerous loss from the night before. What had been a cruise sailed under the protection of the king's flag, was now a perilously slow journey with no obvious deterrent, should men of violent intentions find them struggling at sea. However, he kept this concern to himself while he continued to survey the damage.

In many ways, Declan was grateful as he concluded his walk. He had lost no men, and his family was safe. At his cabin, he called out them, and his wife stepped out first with his young son and daughter following.

"Luke, let me introduce you to my wife, Gwyn." She strode toward Luke with a confidence and elegance not often found in women of Luke's time and place. She offered him her hand, which was as elegant as she was, and Luke bent to kiss it. "He saved my life, and to him I owe a great debt. He is as good as family to me."

Her large eyes sparkled with gratitude. "I thank you stranger. I know not how you were brought to us, but gratitude will be carried with me always when I remember you." Luke thought her voice as beautiful as she was and blushed slightly at her gaze. She continued, "The debt my husband owes you for saving his life is not half what I owe you. He is such a man as few could compare, and I know not what life could offer me should he have been taken last night."

"Children, come forth from behind your mother. You must meet the man whose hands ensured another morning for your father. His name is Luke, and he is to be treated as one of us as often as our paths cross in this life. Luke, these are the apples of my eye. My son, Caedmon, and my daughter, Rhiannon, welcome you."

The young children smiled brightly and said, "Pleasant to meet you, sir," nearly in unison.

"Now that introductions have been made, we have work to do. Men, ready the ship as well we can, port must be made to furnish us with the necessary accoutrements to continue our journey successfully," said Declan directing the men back to work. "Once we are on our way, you men can sleep in shifts to recover from last eve's toil. Unfurl the remaining sails and we shall sail closer to land than has been our wont thus far."

With Declan guiding the ship and the men working to fix what could be repaired at sea, they began to sail in a north-easterly direction. The day was calm, but there was a crisp breeze which caught the remaining sails and provided impetus for quickened speed through the waters. Much of the day passed in this way before land rolled into sight. Declan steered them slowly at an angle that stayed true to their northerly direction but brought them nearer to shore with every league.

As they drew closer, Luke took up a position on the prow and cast his gaze off the starboard side to study the landscape that presented itself. He was amazed at its beauty. Low mountains stretched in the distance, gently sloping toward the sea, ending in dramatic beaches framed by occasional sea cliffs. As the ship continued, the land seemed to recede slightly into a natural bay, shaped like a crescent moon. It was toward this that the boat made way, having passed much of the day trying to sail without the use of a main mast.

Declan steered toward the bay, to weigh anchor for the evening, protected by the natural inlet, bordered on the north by a promontory jutting out into the sea. He was hoping to go ashore the following day to fell a tree to replace the main mast. Declan barked out orders to the men, readying them to stop for the night, to give them all a good rest before resuming their work at the sun's rising the next day.

Within a quarter of an hour after the anchor had found its mark, most of the men were already asleep below. The sun was descending in the west, signaling a clear evening when a keen-eyed sailor espied a ship rounding the corner of the promontory to the north. Declan did not wait to see who was approaching; rather, he roused the men who were at the ready in a mere several minutes, weighing anchor for flight, if needed.

Although the bay was large, it was not so large that the strange ship would not soon be upon the *Gael*. Declan thought the ship rather ominous, as no identifying flag was flying from the mast. Now clear of the promontory and heading into the bay, the ship seemed to be making straight for them. A moment before he turned his head to address the crew, movement from the approaching vessel caught his eye and arrested his attention. A flag was ascending the main mast of the oncoming ship. He stood watching when a look of fearful recognition flashed across his face - a black flag!

"Pirates!!" was the only thing that Declan could transfer from his brain to his mouth before laying hold of the wheel and attempting to swing the *Gael* around. He knew that the unfortunate circumstances of the night before had likely doomed his ship. With no main sail to propel them, they were slow and vulnerable to attack with no royal banner to protect them. His thought was for his family; no loss of material goods was a concern to him now. Rapidly turning the wheel, he was attempting to reach land before the pirates gained the ship. They held no chance of outrunning their pursuers in their crippled condition. Their only hope was to get on solid ground. The pirates could take what they wanted from the ship, as long as his family was safe.

The *Gael* turned, directed by the rudder, but the going was slow, and the other ship was rapidly approaching. They were not far from land, and Declan was trying to calculate the odds of success when a loud explosion broke the silence. A canon had fired from the approaching ship, and the shot flew across the deck of the *Gael*, landing harmlessly in the water. Although the shot had missed its mark, Declan knew that they would not continue to be so fortunate. Grabbing the nearest sailor, the captain explained to him the need to hold the ship steady and steer straight for the shallows.

Luke had been roused with the rest of the men and was working feverishly, helping in whatever way he was capable. When the shot crossed the deck, Luke looked to where Declan had been steering the ship and found him no longer there. Instead, he was loping across the deck, down the stairs and straight toward Luke.

"I am sorry to have put you in this danger," Declan panted. "We are trying to make shore, but that is by no means an assurance. It appears fate was against us in the night, and we are crippled. You are yet a boy and have not yet attained the full stature of manhood. I would have you watch over my family should we be breached. Battle is not for one such as you, if it can be avoided."

Luke moved to respond but another thunderous canon fired, this time crashing through the corner of the aft deck. The damage was limited, but the effect of the hit showed on the faces of the *Gael*'s crew. Declan continued, "It is no safer for my family to hide inside until we are breached, for they can be of use on deck until such time. When I give you the signal, make haste with them into my cabin. You will find arms for protection, should it become necessary. My prayer is that things will not come to that. I see strength in you and have faith that you will do your best when the time comes."

"I will, sir," said Luke. "If I can't fight alongside, I'll do everything I can to keep them safe. You have my word." Declan clasped Luke's hand, his eyes expressing unspoken gratitude.

Declan rallied his men around him, "There is naught to do except man your posts. The *Gael* is wounded, and shore may be beyond our reach. It is likely as not that battle will soon be enjoined. Keep your heads and look to your mates. To arms, and hold steady…"

His words were broken by the final canon blast before the hostile ship pulled alongside the *Gael.* The cannon ball ripped through the hull just above the water line, allowing salty water to splash into the heart of the ship with each wave that slapped the ship's side.

Luke peered across the deck of the *Gael* and into the steely eyes of the criminals that were preparing to board. Shouts and curses were hurled from the enemy ship, swords flashed, and gunfire was exchanged. The sailors of the *Gael* aimed their pistols at the men getting ready to board, while the pirates aimed to defend their mates.

One pirate met Luke's gaze, his face sending a shudder of terror through him. His right eye glared cruelly, but it was the left eye, or lack thereof, that set Luke aback. A dry, black socket was all that remained where his eye should have been, and an ugly scar cut from the middle of the forehead to his left cheekbone showed how the pirate had lost his eye. The man wore faded, but colorful clothes, probably richly made and ripped from a victim, now held in the eternal arms of the ocean. His arms bore grisly scars and ugly tattoos. He lifted his gnarled hand and pointed straight at Luke, who stood paralyzed momentarily, until Declan, rushing with his family, grabbed him by the shoulder.

"Luke, it is time. Go with my family into the cabin, and do not come out. Should we be victorious, I will come get you. Should we suffer a worse fate, arm my family, and defend yourselves. There is good in you, and I hope that you will be alive to witness the rising sun on the morrow. God be with you." With that, Declan gave Luke a gentle but determined shove toward the cabin, his wife and children following close behind.

Luke ran to the cabin door and threw it open. Running as fast as they could, the children crossed the threshold into the cabin, followed directly by their mother, who was protecting them from behind. Luke took one last glance around him only to see the men from the pirate ship fighting to board the

Gael. Declan was in full career toward the railing to defend his ship. Luke grabbed the door handle and dove into the cabin, slamming the door behind him.

Luke expected to hit the floor on the dive, already thinking about the necessity of getting on his feet as quickly as possible, to keep Declan's family safe. But instead of meeting the floor of the cabin, Luke's head crashed against a hard object. He felt a flash of pain, and his world faded into darkness.

11

The Strange File

Dawn broke over the hills of England and shone through a small window at the end of the hall in the ancient house that his parents owned, casting morning light on Luke's face. Luke stirred and opened his eyes groggily. He sat up, leaned against the wall, and rubbed his sore head. He felt a large goose egg, and his head was throbbing slightly. In contrast to the clear light of the morning, his thoughts were cloudy and confused. He could not account for his whereabouts or the pain in his head. He rubbed his eyes and stood up. He quickly leaned back against the wall, as his head felt like it was expanding and contracting. The throbbing almost made him sit back down. He steadied himself, however, closed his eyes, and took a deep breath.

Upon opening his eyes, he saw the door through which he had passed the night before. The maritime carvings pricked his memory. He stood staring at the door for a moment when the goings on of the night before came rushing back to him. This made his head ache even more. He stumbled to the door and threw it open.

A soft light was streaming into the room. The English countryside could be seen through the windows. The furniture was all in order, and the room glowed in the early morning sun. Luke noticed none of this. The *Gael* was gone. Declan and his family were gone. He was home and cursed the magic that had brought him back. Luke's legs buckled, sending him to the floor on his knees. He grabbed his throbbing head, his salty tears falling on the hardwood. Sorrow came on him like waves, as he felt the helplessness of being removed from a desperate situation to which he could not return. He lamented that Declan and his family may have perished.

The tears began to slow, and Luke raised his head from his hands. He slowly stood, steadied himself, and walked into the hallway. He left the house, walking slowly down the hallway, through the front room, and into the open air. Doing so, he started to feel uncomfortable, like there was something about his situation that was problematic, but he could not place it. Once outside, he turned toward his house and suddenly knew the source of the nagging feeling: his parents. How could he explain that he had been out all night and the condition of his forehead?

As he had feared, his parents were in the kitchen eating breakfast. They were surprised to see him walking through the front door and with a bruise on his head. His mother jumped from her seat and ran over to him.

"What happened to your head?!" concern written on her face.

"Oh, it's nothing…," was all Luke could muster.

"Luke, what's going on? Have you been out all night? Are you hurt?" countered Alan.

"Well, I'm…I'm not really sure. I think that I fell asleep in the old house. I must have bumped my head. I woke up in the hallway this morning and came right back."

Alan jumped in, "You must have been sleepwalking again. I wasn't too concerned last time, but this is twice, and you've been hurt this time."

"I'm fine, Dad," Luke stated, trying to minimize what had happened to him, but he knew his parents were not likely to let this pass.

"I'm concerned, dear," Alan said, turning toward Catherine. "I don't want this to be a pattern. Luke, I want you in your room. Rest today. We'll discuss this later; I have to go to work," he stated, again toward his wife.

Luke could see the worry on his parents' faces as he trudged upstairs to his room. He wanted to tell his parents everything - about Ayne, about Declan, about all his dreams. But he knew that they would never understand, much less believe him. If, by some miracle, they did happen to believe him they would be more concerned about his safety in these rooms than the drama that unfolded inside of them. Luke knew that telling his parents everything was not an option. He just hoped that they would not keep him from entering the house again. What he had experienced was not a dream, and the people whom he had met were very real.

* * *

Worn out from his ordeal, his bed looked very welcoming. He pulled the drapes to keep out much of the sun, removed his outer garments and dropped into bed. He had just enough time to slip his hands under his cool pillow and bury his face in it before he was sound asleep.

His sleep was long and dreamless, and he awoke feeling much better. His room was very dark, so he went to the window and pushed the drapes aside. It was a clear night, and the stars shone down resplendently. Luke smiled to think that he had looked up at the same stars under the same sky as Declan. The memory was tinged with sadness, though, as Declan's fate remained unknown.

He glanced at the clock, which showed nearly midnight. Silently, he entered the hallway and crept toward his parent's bedroom, hearing some muffled speech as he approached. Standing with his head near the door, he could make out much of what they were saying. Normally, he would not eavesdrop like this, but he could hear that they were speaking about him.

"I'm concerned. He was hurt this time." Luke recognized his mother's voice.

"I know… me too. I'm just not sure what to do about it. We can't lock our son in his room. If he really is sleepwalking, forbidding him to enter the house at night wouldn't be of much use."

"I keep having this nagging thought that this might have something to do with Luke's history in England. You don't think that he's found anything out, do you?" his mother asked.

"I've been wondering the same thing. I don't know how he could have. He doesn't know where the papers are. I feel bad about not telling him. We've always taught him that honesty was important. I feel like we've lied to him, but I don't know how he would react, especially after all these years."

Luke's heart began thumping as he heard these cryptic words from his father. He had no idea what they could mean, but if he had any thought of returning to his room before the conversation was over, those ideas were now long gone.

"Do you think we should tell him? I mean, he's old enough to understand his own history."

Alan answered, "He didn't look so well this morning. If he's ill, we might want to wait until he's feeling better. Besides, this sleepwalking has me a little worried, and it may not be related to any of this. Still, we should probably work toward telling Luke the truth. We'll let him sleep and see how he is in the morning."

"I think you're right, honey," Catherine said. "I'll get the papers from the safe tomorrow. It's been years since I last looked at them, and I want to make sure that they are all in order when we decide to show them to Luke."

During the last sentence, Luke heard some motion in the room, and he quickly, but silently, backed away from the door. Creeping back to his room, he shut the door, climbed into bed, and pulled the covers over his head. A few moments later, his door creaked slowly open. His parents looked in at their son with a mixture of worry and love on their faces. They eased the door shut and headed back to their bedroom. Luke knew that his parents were going to be sleeping soon, but he had no such designs until he got to the bottom of what his parents were discussing. If there was some secret about him hiding in his father's safe, then he would spend the night discovering what it was. He planned to lie in bed, biding his time until his parents were off to sleep, then he would get up and search for clues to his history.

* * *

Nearly an hour later, Luke was restless in his bed. He wanted to get his hands on his father's safe, but he knew that getting up too early could rouse his parents, especially if they were not completely asleep. He had not heard any noise in over half an hour, so he decided to get out of bed. As quietly as possible, he opened his door and descended the stairs. Every noise that he made seemed amplified, but no sound was forthcoming from his parent's room. His heart steadied a bit when he reached the bottom of the stairs. He moved silently to his father's study and opened the door.

He had seen his parent's safe before but had never given it a second thought. Surely, it held important documents, but he had never considered that his history could be involved. Luke had no idea what secret his parents had been keeping from him, and he was a little afraid of what he might find. His curiosity quickly overcame his fear, and he proceeded into the office.

It was a well-appointed office. Sitting in front of a large window on the far wall was a large mahogany desk. A built-in bookcase covered the wall to his right, with dozens of volumes filling the shelves. A rich oriental rug graced the floor, thick and soft underfoot. Dark wainscoting covered the bottom half of the remaining walls, offsetting the light-colored paint above. None of this concerned Luke that night, however.

His attention was focused on the cabinet at the bottom of the bookcase which housed his father's safe. He opened the doors and carefully pulled it out, placing it on the floor. He tried the safe door, but it was locked. Luke sat for a moment in front of the safe considering where to search for the key. The obvious choice was the desk, and he proceeded to search the drawers for any keys that he could find. He had opened all of the drawers, finding none until he came to the bottom right drawer, which was locked. Luke reopened the main drawer and took out a letter opener, attempting to work the lock with the tool.

Much to his surprise, the lock turned, and he opened the drawer. It was full of miscellaneous papers and rather ordinary looking small books, numerous notepads, and files. He rummaged through the drawer with no success. Several more times he looked to make sure that he had not missed any keys buried amongst the papers. His subsequent efforts were no more successful than his first one. Luke was quickly growing impatient, as he did not want to have to search his father's entire office. It might even be in his parent's room.

He slammed his hand on the side of the drawer in frustration and heard the knock of a solid object against wood.

Luke knew that he had only found paper products in the drawer and wondered what the noise could have been. Repeating the action produced the same sound. This time he emptied the contents to examine it more closely. He shook the drawer and heard something scraping along the bottom. With his hand he felt the inside bottom of the drawer. It appeared solid enough, and pressing it in numerous locations had no effect. He crawled under the desk to examine the drawer, rapped on the bottom, and heard some movement. Applying pressure to different parts of the drawer bottom, he found that it could slide backwards. The drawer had a false bottom! He slid the false bottom off and heard a key drop onto the floor. Scooping up the key, he jumped to the safe.

He was nervous about what he might find but swiftly fit the key and opened the safe. Once again, he found miscellaneous files and papers and had to do some looking before he came across the information for which he was searching. He extricated the file, put the safe back in the cabinet with some effort, placed the key in the false bottom and replaced it in the drawer. As quickly and quietly as he could, he made sure the room was left as he had found it and silently returned to his room. He listened for several minutes to make sure that the house still slept before deciding to open the file.

Sitting at his desk, lit by a small lamp, Luke considered what information the file might soon reveal. He took several deep breaths and fingered the outside of the file before making up his mind to open it. Inside, he found a sealed manila envelope. He paused for a moment to consider the risks of opening the envelope, as his parents would know that someone had tampered with it. Curiosity overcame his caution, and he slipped his finger under the flap and ripped across the top.

Luke pulled out its contents and emptied them on his desk. There were several official-looking papers and one very yellowed, looking much older than the rest. This document piqued his curiosity; he set aside the other papers and focused his attention on the antique document and read its contents.

12

The Princess

Luke was too shocked to know what to do. He couldn't think. His head was spinning, and he could not sequence his thoughts. He felt hot, the air thick around him. His breathing became labored and sweat began to trickle down his back. He had never had a panic attack before, but knew he was about to experience one if he did not do something soon. Dashing out of his room, Luke flew down the stairs and out the front door, not even bothering to close the door behind him. He stopped for a moment, feeling the cool night breeze on his face. He desperately needed to get away, to think, and he knew just where to go to get his mind off what he had learned. Redoubling his speed, he headed for the stone building next door. There were yet several doors that could take him far away from here.

He entered the house unceremoniously, dashing through the front door. At the back hallway he stopped. He had been in two rooms already, and both experiences had ended badly. Luke knew that only trouble was to be found through those doors, and he was in little condition to effect any change in the situations as they were when he had left. Choosing the first door on the left, he stepped through, barely taking the time to notice the intricate medieval carvings on the door as he passed by.

The room was dark but for a flickering light that was the product of a small fire in a fireplace at the far left end of the room. Luke remembered there had been a fireplace in the medieval room but this one seemed farther away than he thought it should have been. The room he was standing in was larger than the one in the house. It had worked. He was in a different place than he had been on the other side of the door.

Luke was just about to move around the room when he heard a sound coming from his right. He froze, not wanting to move until he discerned the source of the sound. Slowly turning his head, he saw a massive bed. The bedposts were thicker than he had ever seen in his life, about the thickness of a man's leg. The posts must have been ten feet tall, all four connected at the top by thin planks. Delicate fabric was draped over these planks, which swirled down around the posts themselves. Fabric of the same kind also hung down like giant curtains on each side of the bed, hiding the source of the noise behind them.

Being unseen and unsure of his next move, Luke looked about the room. It was a large, circular room, but it had only one window. The window was taller than it was wide and had a pointed arch at the top. It had a stone pane bisecting the window, which split to the left and right as it entered the arch. A faint, blue light entered the glassless window as the moon made its course across the night sky. The light from the fire and the pale moonlight made it possible to get a good impression of the room, although fine details were difficult to make out.

The small fire burned in an imposing stone hearth. A large, dark tapestry adorned the wall above the fireplace. It appeared to be a magnificent piece of artistry, depicting a hunting scene, although the darkened room and years of soot conspired to dull the colors. A thick rug softened the hard floor in front of the fireplace and spilled into the center of the room. The rug was identical in form to the one in the old house but thicker and somehow more vibrant. The family crest adorned the wall by which Luke stood, protected on either side by swords, gleaming in the reflected light of the flickering fire. Luke was stunned to see that the crest matched precisely with Declan's family flag that had been hoisted atop the mainsail. A chest held a position near the window on the opposite wall and appeared very similar to the chest in the stone house. This one too appeared locked.

Two empty chairs were positioned in front of the fire, and an intricately carved wooden writing table was stationed just to the left of the window, affording its user a glimpse of the goings on outside of the castle. Beside these, the room contained little else.

The noise continued from behind the curtains of the bed. Luke crept closer to discover its nature. As he drew nearer, he discerned the muffled sound of crying. The voice sounded feminine and young - and distressed. Stepping closer, Luke disrupted an empty bedpan that was lying on the floor.

The crying immediately ceased, and a shaky voice called out, "Who goes there?"

Luke remained completely still, not moving a muscle and not daring to breathe. His mind raced in an effort to discover his next move. His heart pounded so hard, he was afraid its noise would give him away.

A moment of tense silence gave way before a tear-streaked face emerged from between the folds of fabric surrounding the bed.

"Who might you be? Speak quickly or I shall call my guards. They stand close at hand, ready to protect me."

"My…my name is…my name is Luke. I… I'm not sure how…I'm really sorry. I did not mean to intrude. Please, I don't mean you any harm. I think this is just a big mistake. I should leave now." Luke began backing away from the bed toward the door.

"Halt," she commanded softly but firmly. "Do not take one more step, or I shall scream. I intend to discover your purpose in my bedchamber. It does not become you to approach me in my bed by way of stealth. And how did you get past the guards standing at the ready outside my door?"

In an instant, a dozen different responses flitted across Luke's mind, but before he could stop himself, he blurted out the truth. He told her of the house and entering the door only to find himself in her room.

"I have heard of such passages, but how am I to know you speak the truth, stranger?" she questioned.

"This is not the first time I have been in another place through that house," Luke replied. "I have been in a place before time as we know it, witnessing the last of a dying race, and I have seen a place in time that has not yet come for you, watching a noble family being kidnapped by pirates."

"I would hear more of this," she replied, as she stepped from the bed and wiped the tears from her face. "Let us repose by the fire."

Luke proceeded to tell her about his adventures with Ayne and Declan. "You know of Ayne?" the girl's eyes grew wide, as she interrupted the story. "There are very few who know that name anymore. I will know you speak the truth if you tell me the title by which he is known."

"He is known as Ayne the Last," Luke replied with sadness in his eyes. "He was good to me, and I've thought of him often since then. He suffered the loss of his family, his people, and his world. He was the last of a good and dying kind, and I was not with him at the end."

"This is truly amazing," she gasped. "Even fewer are the number who know to tell of him as you have described. Could it be that you speak the truth?"

"I wouldn't lie to you. If my plan was to lie to you, I would choose something that was more believable. Besides, you asked yourself how I was able to get past your guards. I was never in the hall outside your door, just in your room."

"I am glad to have company, tonight of all nights. Please, continue with your tales, and leave nothing out."

Luke continued with his story, the girl across from him gazing in rapt attention as he told his tales.

"…and that is how I came to be in your room," Luke concluded, leaving out the details of his own world.

"You have such stories to tell," she said before her countenance suddenly changed. "I must beg your forgiveness. I have made you tell me much, and I have not made introductions. You have said that your name is Luke. My name is Alexis. I am a princess in this realm. I am daughter to King…" Her voice trailed off and tears began welling in her eyes. "I was daughter to King Cyric." She paused, tears choking her voice. She valiantly tried to contain herself, but her sorrow broke forth, and she buried her face in her hands as waves of grief shook her.

Luke could but watch as she sobbed in front of the fire. The light danced on her fine dark hair, which fell freely down her back. Her simple white gown shimmered, as if strands of silver had been woven through it. She appeared to be roughly the same age as Luke, if not a little older. Her delicate, white hands cradled her head as she fought to regain composure.

"I am sorry for the way I have acted. I have made a fool of myself."

The few tears that had not fled her eyes caught the light of the fire, causing her brown eyes to sparkle. Her cheek was fair and her look noble. Her tears endeared her to Luke, who wanted nothing more than to comfort her.

"You have no need to be sorry, princess," Luke responded. "Why are you crying?"

"My father, the king, no longer walks among us. We received word of his death not three days ago. They say he died in battle, but this I doubt."

"What do you think happened?"

"My father's sister was given in marriage to a malcontent lord. He is a usurper but is subtle and wily in his ways. I believe that my father's death was no accident. Neither do I believe it accidental that this man is now steward of the kingdom until I marry and receive a king. He is forcing me to marry is his own vile son!" Anger delayed the tears for a moment before they broke forth again, burying her head in her hands once more. "I do not know what to do. My father always knew what to do, but he is no longer here…But enough of this sadness." Pulling herself together, she continued, "We will talk of happier things while you are sojourning with me."

"Princess," Luke began.

"Please, call me Alexis," she interrupted.

"Alexis, please tell me about your father. What kind of king was he? What fond memories do you have of him?"

"My fondest memory…" she mused with a sad smile of reminiscence. "I will tell you a story if you will listen. It is one my father used to tell me. I have heard it often enough to remember every word. I have loved the hearing of it, now I will learn to love the telling. Will you listen to my tale?"

"Please," encouraged Luke.

"Before going to battle, my father would tell me this story. He said it was to help calm my fears, but I think it calmed him too. I think he gained strength from its telling. I was his only child, and he loved me all the more for it. He said he needed no sons for having such a daughter. Indeed, he said it was only to me he could tell this story, for none other in his realm was worthy."

She paused, gathering her breath, and continued. "In ages past, when skies were clearer, the earth was richer, and water was purer, there lived a High King, who established himself over the peoples of the land. He was a good king, whose justice and benevolence won him the fealty of surrounding lords and chieftains. There was peace in his time and prosperity marked his reign.

"A mighty caer was built of wood and stone to honor his place in the kingdom. A worthy hill was chosen, and his seat was established upon it. No caer in the land resembled its likeness, none its grandeur. Sedd o Daioni was its name, and it was the jewel of his kingdom. Great walls were constructed at different levels, with staggered gates to thwart invaders. Within the first wall were merchants selling fine wares and grocers selling foods harvested from the fields without. A visitor to the land may not have ever seen cloth so fine or tasted fruit so sweet as was found within the outer wall. Within the next wall, more merchants were to be found, selling finer wares and more succulent food. Each level was better than the last, demonstrating the wonder of the kingdom. Within the highest walls lived the High King.

"His great majesty was displayed within these walls, and no place was greater than the Hall of Kings. This hall was built entirely of grey stone, harvested from the earth for none other than his mighty hall. Its height was greater than ten men standing on top of one another. It housed the king, his family, and the royal servants. There were more than fifty private chambers, and the banquet hall could host more than thrice one hundred warriors.

"Despite the greatness of the Hall of Kings, the High King loved a nobler form of greatness. His joy was not fulfilled with Sedd o Daioni nor was it expressed with the Hall of Kings. The High King was driven by a higher purpose; he served the God of Heaven, the Bestower of Good, the Sovereign of Sovereigns. The High King knew that he served a higher King and was but his humble servant.

"A royal chapel was built, and this the king cherished. It was plain and small, completely encircled by a stone wall higher than the tallest man in the kingdom. There was but one gate in. Beautiful gardens could be found within its walls, flowers blooming continually in the warm seasons. Flowering trees could be found at regular intervals, and large, leafy trees provided ample shade, casting emerald light on the lawn below as the sun shone through the leaves.

"The king could often be found walking in those gardens or making supplication in the chapel. The little church was simple, yet beautiful. The stone of the chapel represented strength. Its simplicity represented the king's humility. Beautiful colored glass windows were placed on the eastern and western side of the chapel to illumine the little church. The king called upon the Almighty One each sunrise to bless the toil of his people and each sunset to comfort the same in their beds.

"Plain wooden benches rested three deep on each side of the stone aisle in the center. The aisle led to a small dais, on which an altar was found. Fine crimson cloth covered the altar, upon which a golden cross stood. Candles burning in sconces on the walls cast their flickering light upon the cross, dancing across the polished gold.

"Although the High King loved his chapel and gardens more than any other place in his realm, he felt that his dedication and service to the Holy One was lacking a physical symbol that would inspire his people to belief and greater works. He coveted a holy relic. He had heard rumors of holy relics nearly his entire life. Oh, how pilgrims would flock to Sedd o Daioni if he could but obtain the Crown of Thorns, the True Cross, or even the Cup of Christ itself, the Sangreal.

"The king became consumed with blessing his kingdom with a holy relic, but he knew that he could not search it out himself. He would be neglecting his kingship should he leave his kingdom in search of something that he may never find.

"The king might have despaired of ever finding the desire of his heart had not his beautiful queen borne him two extraordinary sons. They were twins; Lew and Lewis were their names. The brothers grew strong of mind and body and wanted nothing more than to honor their father and the All Knowing by obtaining a holy relic. When eighteen summers had passed over them, the twins set out on a journey far and wide, wandering far outside of the realms of the High King, in search of their holy prize.

"In spite of the holy purpose of the journey and the love shared between the brothers, their endeavor began to wear upon them. The brothers did not share the same vision for procuring the symbol of the Christ. Lew sought out sacred places, constantly lifting his petition to the All Seeing to aid him in his search. Lewis sought out war and battle. He thought to win the relic through might of arms, eventually forsaking divine guidance in his search.

"The brothers parted, Lew praying for his brother's soul, and Lewis shunning his brother's weakness. Lew's heart was pained at his brother's departure. Lewis now felt unencumbered in his search.

"Lew and Lewis searched for three and ten years with no success. As those years passed, Lew spent more and more time in prayer, seeking the guidance of the Giver of Gifts, while Lewis forsook his original purpose. He turned to amassing fame and fortune in battle. His desires became base, and he sought only to serve his flesh.

"However, the brothers were destined to reunite. Lewis had formed a battle band raiding a town many days journey from his father's lands. The town was unsuspecting and the band quick and deadly. None of the townspeople lived to see the sun finish its celestial course. As the raiders were sacking the town, Lewis entered the town's small chapel to carry off anything of value. Movement at the front of the church caught his eye. It appeared that a single soul had escaped the wrath of his war band. Lewis unsheathed a knife from his waist and sent it sailing toward the other in the church. His aim was deadly, the blade piercing the heart of the stranger. Lewis ran forward to glory in his kill only to find his brother, Lew, gasping for his last breaths. In his hand was the Crown of Thorns. Lewis had murdered his brother, who died holding the earthly crown of the Christ in his hand. The sin of Lewis overpowered him, and he fell to his knees. He held the relic in his hands and lifted his voice to the Father of Forgiveness to cleanse his soul. He clenched his fists in anger and despair, driving the thorns into his hands.

"His path lay clear before him. His suffering was mixed with that of the Christ's. He prayed that his hands would not heal as a symbol of his penance until he returned to his father's kingdom with the relic. From that day forward, Lewis forsook wealth and glory. He donned nothing but a brown robe secured with a rope belt. His feet were bare and grew calloused on his journey home. The Spirit of Righteousness granted his petition and his hands seeped blood until he arrived at his father's gate one year to the day of the death of Lew.

"Lewis hid nothing from his father, telling of his great sins and the murder of his brother. He spoke of his forgiveness and the penance that he was granted. When Lewis presented his father with the Crown of Thorns, the blood had already stopped flowing, the wounds having closed on his hands. Lewis left Sedd o Daioni that same day, forsaking his royal heritage. Father and sons paid a high price for the holy relic.

"The Keeper of Light did not long withhold his blessing from the High King, however. Sedd o Daioni soon became much more than a monument to the great king. It became a sacred place, becoming even more blessed than it had been before. Lewis also prospered, but in a much different way. His life was dedicated to prayer and worship. He built a small chapel in a wooded glen, honoring the Lord of Life, giving all he had to the poor and needy of the country. He became a man of some renown, as each year on the anniversary of his brother's death, his hands would begin bleeding and would continue to bleed from the moment the sun's rays began warming the earth until the last ray disappeared behind the horizon, a yearly reminder of the penance he owed. Despite the suffering this caused Lewis, he gladly bore it, for on this day he could heal the sick with a single drop of his blood. People flocked to him from all over the land, and he performed many miracles, gladly bleeding to restore life where he had once taken it.

"Each year he bled less and less and grew weaker and weaker on the day of his penance. His blood loss sapped his life and his strength, but he continued to serve and to heal for five and twenty years when one morning, on the day of his penance, he did not rise from his bed. His followers found his bed empty with but a single blood red rose lying where he had been. The rose was buried outside of the chapel in a humble grave in lieu of Lewis' missing body. Later that year was found a rose bush growing from the site of the holy man's grave that produced but a single rose each year. The rose was blood red and more beautiful than any in the realm of the High King.

"The Rose of Saint Lewis is on my family's crest, and he is this kingdom's patron saint. Thus concludes my story, and ever will I fondly remember my father in its telling. Oh, that the Saint could heal the wrongs lately committed against my father and soon to be forced upon me."

Her voice trailed off with these words and silence reigned for a moment before the darkness lifted from her eyes. "My worries are mine own, and not yours to bear. I would show you as much of my father's kingdom as the cover of night would allow were it not for the guards outside of my door."

As she spoke these words, a sparkle gleamed in her eye, she pursed her lips, and knit her brow in thought. "We can use the fabric of my bed to lower ourselves out of my window, if you are willing."

"I am willing," replied Luke, eager to explore with the young princess. They took to their project with a will and soon found themselves on the turf twenty feet below her window.

13

Escape

The night was radiant, dazzling stars pronouncing an end to the day. Bright pinpricks of light fell from the moonless sky. Crickets sang their night-song; an owl hooted a reminder of its presence to the visitors. The air was crisp but not cold, the turf springy beneath their feet.

Alexis took Luke by the hand and led him away from the caer, striding gracefully across the lawn. After a score of paces, Luke turned to look at the castle. The wood and stone structure loomed nearly forty feet high. The princess' room was on a corner of the castle, which was a nicely rounded tower with a vaulted, conical ceiling. The curtain walls of the caer ran away from Luke for at least one hundred feet before turning again to complete the square. The facade of the castle was rather plain but spoke of strength and nobility.

Not wanting to waste any time, Alexis pulled on Luke's hand, "Let us ride tonight. The royal stables hold such beautiful horses, and a starlit ride will lift my spirits."

Luke began to protest, "Princess Alexis, I've only ridden a horse several times. I don't know that I can do this."

"You will do well," she returned with a sparkle in her eye. "You have never ridden such horses as these, and I will guide you."

Luke was unsure, but each step brought him nearer to the stables and Alexis' horses. They had been traveling in the shadows of the castle, lurking to avoid detection. Near the end of the wall, a door appeared. Alexis tightened her grip on Luke's hand and ran for the door. He followed closely behind as they flattened themselves against the wall.

"This leads into the courtyard next to the stables. There should be no one to interfere at this time of night. We shall grab each horse's tether and lead them through this door. We must make haste and will have no time to saddle. We will ride like the warriors of old," she said, flashing a bright smile.

Alexis unlocked the door and led Luke inside. He was amazed to see that the courtyard encompassed nearly half of the inside of the caer's walls. Livestock pens lined the wall they had just entered. What appeared to be a granary or storehouse took up much of the opposite wall. To his right was the main entrance to the courtyard, a double door large enough for two wagons to enter abreast. The doors were flanked by towers, each containing a gatehouse. Parapets lined the walls, affording defenders a strategic position. To his left was the entrance to the keep with a significantly smaller set of double doors, although a single wagon could still fit through. The walls of the castle rose to twice the height of the curtain walls and were filled with windows, bespeaking the large number of rooms the structure contained. Parapets were also found atop the main building for defense, should the gates be breached. Spotty grass covered the ground. It was evident that much foot traffic, both human and animal, kept the grass from growing thickly in the courtyard.

He was quickly led to the stables, where Alexis took him to two beautiful mares tethered in their stalls, chomping peacefully on the remnants of their hay. The horses were untethered and squeezed through the doorway and outside the courtyard walls. Alexis locked the door and quickly led them away into the woods. She struck upon a trail and mounted her horse when they had gained some measure of cover.

"Grab the mane and throw your leg over your horse's back. Stay low to the horse as you slide on."

Luke made several vain attempts before finally mounting, almost falling off as his horse shifted her footing. "I don't know if I can do this, Alexis. I have never ridden bareback before."

"Squeeze tightly with your knees. That will keep you in place. Lean forward and grip her mane lightly. You will find that horses such as my father bred do not easily throw their riders. Let it not be said that Luke, companion of Ayne the Last, displayed less courage than a young princess this night." At which she kicked her heels and galloped through the woods.

Unsure of how to proceed, Luke imitated the princess and kicked his heels into the horse's flanks. His mount bolted down the path with frightening speed. Luke's riding lessons had not gotten to maneuvering the horse, but fortunately it followed the princess down the trail and through the woods.

Soon the wood grew thinner, and a meadow opened before them. The horses flew through the long grass, which whipped at the legs of the riders. The fresh, clear, air filled Luke's lungs, sending a thrill through his body. Flying on the back of the horse, Luke thought he knew what it must be like for the wind to blow free across the open fields. The breeze rustled his hair, and he released his grip on the horse's mane. He spread his arms wide, enveloping the night sky and threw his head back, letting out a yell of exhilaration.

Hearing his shout, Alexis quickly slowed her horse, causing Luke's to do the same. He almost lost his balance and pulled himself back close to his horse, disappointed that the run was over. "You must stay quiet. It is unwise to wake anyone."

"Who would be around to hear us?" Luke wondered out loud. "We must be several miles from the castle by now."

"It is not those within the castle of whom I speak," she returned. "We are not far from a small village of peasants that work my father's fields. I would show you those who will be under my stewardship."

They approached a thin line of trees creating the eastern boundary of the field. "We must tether our horses in these trees and proceed on foot. We cannot alert the peasants to our presence."

With that, Alexis slipped from her horse and tied it to a tree. Luke did the same, although less gracefully. The horses contented themselves with the grass growing at the foot of the trees, as the princess and Luke walked through the thicket and into a large clearing on the other side.

A huddle of huts emerged in the night as they approached the small settlement. Several sensations met Luke simultaneously as the dwellings grew nearer. An acrid odor began to fill his nostrils. Human and animal stench wafted from the dwellings toward him. He was also struck by the squalid nature of the dwellings. They were small, round huts, framed with wood, filled in with mud, and roofed with thatch. There were no people to be seen, but a few dirty animals milled about.

The cry of a baby pierced the night, sickly and shrill. It came from a hut near them. Luke and Alexis slowly approached the hut from behind, so as not to be seen. The baby whimpered from within while another voice joined it. A widow's prayer was offered up for her sickly child. The voice was strained from crying, unsure of how to care for her little one.

"We must go in and comfort this woman. I know too well the pain of loss. If I am to be queen, I must help the people."

She entered the open doorway of the hut, with Luke following close behind. The floors were dirt, bearing up a single bed of moldy hay upon which the mother and child lay. A few wooden tools were found about the hut, along with cooking implements. Otherwise, the hut was bare. Abject poverty characterized the peasants who were at the mercy of the lord they served and elements in which they lived.

The woman, filthy and smelly, had not yet reached her twenty-fifth year of life, yet she appeared frail and bent, dried skin hung on the frame of what appeared to be a much older woman. The child was small and within its first year of life, struggling to eat, struggling to sleep, struggling to live.

Alexis was moved and proceeded to the bed of hay. She lifted the babe into her arms as her eyes filled with tears. "I am here to help. Take courage; tonight you will both rest." She turned to Luke and spoke decidedly, "Stay with them. I will return shortly." She returned the baby to the bed, grabbed a small pot, and quickly left the dwelling. She was gone but five minutes, returning with a water-filled pot and some herbs. She expertly ground the herbs into a powder and mixed them into the water. She bade the mother drink the admixture and then gave some to the whimpering child.

Alexis again picked up the child, holding it as if it were her own. She spoke soothingly to the mother, reassuring her as best she could, lulling the woman into a relaxed state. The child was soon asleep, as evidenced by her slow, regular breathing. The mother's brow relaxed, her eyes closed, and she too was soon asleep. Alexis lay the sleeping babe across her mother's chest and led Luke from the hut.

"You were amazing, like an angel of mercy to these poor people."

"My father had a heart for the people, but he was often away protecting the land. Those who ruled in his stead saw the people of this land as mere vessels for their own use. I fear the same is true for the Steward and his son, the one he would have me marry." Disgust crept across her face as she spoke of them. "I would care for these people. I would heal their hurts and bring them happiness. They deserve better than this squalor."

Tears began to fill her eyes as she considered the plight of her subjects. "I cannot marry the Steward's son. I cannot return to my home. Without my father, it is just a castle. I have an uncle who wields no small power in this land. I will flee to him until I can right the wrongs that have been committed."

"Can you do this?" wondered Luke, his voice cut with concern. "How far away is it?"

"It is a two day's ride. My father taught me much. I can find food and rest in the land. If I leave tonight, I will have a head start even the best riders will not overcome."

Luke's thoughts began to turn to himself. With his previous experiences, he knew that he would have to go back to Alexis' room to get back to his own world. "Princess, I have to go back, and I am not sure of my way. I know it could be risky for you to return with me, but I need your help to get back."

"I shall return with you," she replied. "You have done much for me this night. When you arrived in my room, I was afraid and comforting myself with tears. Now I am emboldened and will comfort myself with action. I cannot honor my father or these people with fear. Let us return quickly."

She led Luke to the horses. They untied them, mounted, and rode off through the night, the stars as their guides, back to the caer. As they approached the castle, they noticed some movement outside the walls.

"My absence has been discovered. This bodes ill for both of us. I dare not leave the cover of the wood. I fear that your horse will give you away. Your return may not be discovered if you make your way quickly on foot. It will not take you long to cover the ground from here to the wall. Just take care that you are not seen."

Luke slipped from his horse, tied it to a sturdy tree, and approached Alexis. "I am very glad to have met you. May God be with you on your journey. He lifted the princess' hand from her horse and bent to kiss it. He paused in surprise when he saw a ring upon her finger. It was identical to the one on the hands of Ayne and Declan.

"Where did you get this ring? I have seen it before."

"It is an heirloom, a token of my family. My father gave it to me before he left me for the last time. It has been passed down in my family from time before my grandfather's grandfather."

Her statement warmed Luke with hope. Could it be that a descendant of Ayne survived? Could it be that she was the mother of Declan's family line? He had little time to contemplate the possibilities before circumstances demanded his action.

"You must go," Alexis urged him. "Time will only bring more searchers."

Luke kissed her hand, their eyes exchanging a glance of mutual admiration. Creeping from the wood line, he had not gained a score of paces before the press was upon him. He was spotted, and guards engaged him in pursuit. Toward the castle he surged and spied the window to Alexis' room. The linens still hung from the window, urging Luke on faster. Desperation drove his speed, and he reached the makeshift rope about ten steps ahead of his nearest pursuer. He leaped to grab the linens as high as he could reach, quickly pinching the rope between his feet and pushing himself upwards. He was halfway toward the window when he noticed that no one was following him up the side of the castle. This did not diminish his speed, however, as he soon reached the window. He was about to grab the ledge to pull himself in, when he heard some voices inside the room.

"Seize him," sounded a husky voice. Large hands shot through the window, grabbing Luke by the shirt and arms, pulling him through. Torches illuminated the room as a dozen guards stood menacingly. A large, dark-looking man stepped from the shadows. He was richly dressed and wore a snarl on his face. "Where is the princess? Answer carefully if you value your life."

"The princess is beyond your grasp now." Almost before the words were out of his mouth, the man rained a crushing blow to Luke's face, crumpling him to his knees. The room was blurred in front of him, and pain seared through his head.

"Take him away. He will be talking shortly." A pair of guards approached Luke and began dragging him toward the door. Too dazed to gain his footing, his feet trailed out behind him. A third guard threw open the door, and as they dragged Luke across the threshold he fell from their arms. He lay crumpled in the hallway of the ancient house next to his home. The desire to sleep off the headache overtook him, and he slept the night away on the hard, wooden floor.

14

The Truth

The rising sun found Luke slumped in the hallway of the old house. He dozed silently, recovering from a difficult night. He might have slept on had he not been disturbed by his environment. The hardness of the floor reminded his body that he was not in his own bed. The realization that he had been sleeping in a strange place suddenly snapped Luke into consciousness. Sleep! The reality crept into Luke's mind like an unwanted stranger.

Despite the remnants of a headache, he realized that he had every intention of returning to his room the night before and replacing the documents that he had removed. He was cursing himself for falling asleep in the hallway and not returning home. He arose and left the house, stepping out into the morning sun. The dew wet his shoes as he crossed the lawn to his own front door.

He quietly opened the door and listened. Voices and shuffling paper emanated from his father's office. He knew the commotion was from his parents attempting to locate the documents. He crept up to his room to gather the papers. He was going to be discovered, and he decided to face it manfully. He organized the papers, put them under his arm and descended the stairs.

Words drifted to Luke as he approached his father's office, "I told you. I don't know where they could be. I know I put them in here."

"Are you sure? Papers don't just get up and walk away." Luke recognized the voice as his mother's, and he knew how his father hated it when his mother was condescending.

"Well, apparently they must have, because I put them in here," retorted Alan in frustration.

Luke peered around the corner of the doorway to see his father wearing a scowl, his shirt sleeves pushed back, kneeling on the floor with papers all around him. His mother was standing over his father scrutinizing the search. Her look was also one of frustration, but it was aimed at Alan for losing such important documents.

"You won't find them in there," broke in Luke.

His parents looked startled. They did not expect to see Luke at such an early hour, and his words confused them.

"What are you talking about, son?" asked Alan.

"I have what you're looking for," he replied.

"How do *you* know what we're looking for?" Catherine wondered out loud.

"I'm sorry, but I heard you two talking last night, and I had to see for myself. Is this true? Are these papers about me?"

Luke's parents glanced mutely at one another, both waiting for the other to begin. A moment later, Alan cleared his throat and started.

"You weren't supposed to see those. Um… well, I didn't mean it like that. You *were* supposed to see those. Er… I mean, we were going to tell you. This isn't an easy thing, son. I…you see, your mother and I thought…. Look, this is a difficult thing to just talk about. We meant to tell you…," his voice trailed off, and he took a deep breath.

"Let me start over. Luke, you know we love you, and we always want to be honest with you. We meant to tell you a long time ago, and we were waiting for a time when you were old enough to really understand. Then one day, we realized that you were old enough, and we were concerned that you had quickly passed from not being old enough to understand your history to being too old to understand why we kept it from you for so long. We were waiting for the right time, but I guess it never seemed right. We never meant for you to find out like this. I'm so sorry."

Luke was hurt. He was hurt that those years of the only reality that he had ever known had been shattered in one night. He was angry that his parents had not trusted him with vital information about his past. He was confused about what this meant for his future. He felt alone, his parents suddenly appearing to him like guilty strangers.

"Honey, you're right to be upset. But we love you. We have loved you from the beginning. We will love you until the end. You are no different to us than if we had one of our own. I know this is hard for you and may take a while to process. Please come in. I guess now is the right time. We'll tell you everything we know." His mother's eyes looked both guilty and pleading.

"I want to know the truth; I think I deserve it." Luke's voice was calm but firm.

"Luke," started his father, "we were told by doctors long ago that we couldn't have children. We tried for years with no success. We decided that we wanted to adopt before we felt too old to be raising children. So, we adopted you. It was a strange adoption, to be sure. We tried to go the normal route, but it was very expensive and took a lot of time. I had recently found out about my transfer to the U.S., and we wanted to start our new life with a family. Things were progressing slowly, and we were afraid that we would have to start all over again in the States.

"Then one morning, we found you on our steps. You looked like you were only several days old. You were wrapped in old blankets with no clothes on underneath them. You had a brown string tied around your little wrist with that bit of old parchment rolled up and fastened to the string."

Luke interjected, "There's only one word on it, and I've never seen anything like it before. What does it mean?" He took out the small piece of parchment and exposed the word to his parents.

The single word was written in a fine hand, the ink having faded to brown, and was centered in the middle of the paper. Luke thought the word strange and intriguing.

"Disgynnydd," said Alan. "We researched it as soon as we found it. It is Welsh, an ancient Celtic language, and it means 'descendant'. It was very strange. We never found out who left you or the reason behind the single word."

"It seemed too good to be true," spoke up his mother. "We took it as a sign of providence. We had no way of having children, descendants, and here you were on our front step with a paper saying that you were a descendant. It's a long story, but as they could find no one to claim you, we were able to adopt you. We came to the U.S. as a family. We have loved you no differently than if you were naturally ours."

"There was something else attached to the string," Alan interposed. He got up from his knees and shuffled through the remaining papers in the safe. His face declared when he found his prize. He clasped the object in his hand and stood to face Luke.

"We also found this." He opened his hand to expose the object.

Luke's jaw dropped in amazement, rendering him momentarily speechless. His parents were surprised to see the look on Luke's face.

"Do you know what this is? Why do you look so surprised to see this?" asked Alan.

"I…I…I don't know what to say," Luke stuttered. He was so perplexed and amazed that he could hardly form words. He was suddenly grateful for his temporary difficulty with speech. Would his parents understand his adventures in the old house? Would they even believe him? He instantly decided to keep his nocturnal travels to himself. "I guess I'm just surprised that something like that was with me. It's so strange, you have to admit. Do you know where it came from?" Luke figured that a question might sidetrack his parents and allow time to compose himself, hopefully avoiding any more questions about his initial response.

"We took it to several experts," Catherine said. "Most of them said that it was the oldest piece of jewelry they had ever seen, some offered a huge amount of money for it, and none had any idea of its origins. We could have sold it and lived a much different life, but it is tied to you in some way, and we could not part with it. It is yours by rights, and we want you to have it."

Alan continued, "We have kept this from you long enough. This ring and what you hold are all that we have of your history. You hold your adoption papers and the old bit of parchment. You can keep all of these in your possession. Son, this ring is special and very valuable. There are many who would like it for research or for greed. You will eventually have to decide as to what you want to do with it. We can keep it safe for you in here if you'd like."

"No," Luke stated thoughtfully. "I'd like to keep it in my room."

"Keep it safe," his mother cautioned.

Luke knew that those words had no need to be spoken. "I will keep it safe. It is part of who I am, and I'd like to find out how it is connected to me."

Alan carefully placed the ring on the desk, and Luke stepped forward. He grasped the ring and turned to leave the room. His voice trailed away as he walked up the stairs, "I'd like to be alone in my room for a while…"

* * *

Luke sat at his desk pondering the abrupt change in his life. His emotions were conflicted and his thoughts racing. He was angry with his parents for allowing him to believe a lie. He felt sympathy for the plight of his parents and their difficulty having children. He was confused about his origins, and he wanted to get back into the old house as soon as the cover of night would allow.

He fingered his ring, tracing the yellow lines with his fingernails across its surface. The ring was in exquisite condition and identical to the one he had seen on Ayne, Declan, and Alexis. It looked newly forged and had not so much as a scratch on it. Luke marveled at the ring and wondered if it could be the very same ring he had seen. It did not seem possible but neither did most of the adventures he had survived.

His thoughts turned to the remaining doors. He had some portent of what would be in the third carved door in the hallway. He had visited it in his dreams and had seen the room with the aid of daylight. He yearned to see what answers would be discovered when he crossed its threshold.

Though he had given it little thought previously, he suddenly remembered the fourth door in the hallway. It had been very plain, less enticing than the other doors, but he had no clue what lay behind it. He had no idea what secrets it contained. No dream had given him glimpses, and the door seemed impenetrable. There was no way of knowing what awaited him on the other side of the door.

Thus far, he had progressed through the doors in the same order as he had in his dreams, and he was determined to continue the pattern. He had no luck opening the plain door previously and hoped that the third door would provide some clue to the mystery of the locked one. He was itching to continue his exploration, but his throbbing head was a painful reminder of his most recent narrow escape and his need to recuperate.

Luke held the ring a moment longer, staring at the possibilities it burned into his brain. He slipped the ring onto his left forefinger and found that it fit him perfectly. Holding out his hand, he examined the ring. He felt soothed by it and allowed his muscles to relax, suddenly realizing how tired he was. Slowly he got up, made his way to his bed and lay down. The cool pillow and soft sheets welcomed him and cradled him to sleep.

What seemed a short while later, Luke's eyes flitted open. Wakefulness crept over him like a warm glow. He propped himself up on one elbow, surprised to have a clear head and supple muscles. All the earlier soreness had dissipated, and he felt well and strong. Luke glanced at the clock, which told him that he had slept most of the day. Only about an hour of sunlight remained, the light already waning slightly through his window.

He climbed out of bed, quickly took a shower, and put on some clean clothes. He glanced at his hand, smiling in wonder at the ring that he wore. Down the stairs and to the first floor Luke went in search of dinner. He felt like he had not eaten for days and was looking forward to sustenance. Almost as soon as he entered the kitchen, his parents stood up and came to him.

"Are you feeling alright?" wondered Catherine, concern written across her face.

"Yeah, I'm feeling fine," replied Luke a little quizzically.

"Are you sure, son? You've been out for quite a while," Alan interjected.

"I'm fine," Luke repeated. "I just took a long nap. I know you're worried about me with what you told me this morning, but I was just tired, that's all."

"This morning?" asked Alan. "Luke, that was yesterday. You have been asleep for more than a day! We checked in on you periodically and tried to wake you once or twice, but you were very sound asleep, so we let you lie. We were starting to get worried."

"You're kidding," Luke shot back. "I couldn't have been asleep for that long."

"Look at the newspaper," Alan added.

Luke picked up the paper, and indeed it was later than it should have been. Luke shook his head in disbelief as he stood in the entrance to the kitchen.

"Son, come in. You've got to be hungry. I cooked supper, and it should still be warm," his mother offered.

Luke sat down and managed to eat what was put in front of him, although without conviction. He had a far off look in his eye, as he was trying to wrap his mind around the fact that he had been asleep since yesterday morning.

"I think I'm going to go for a walk. I'll probably be gone for a little while. I don't think I'll be tired any time soon."

"Don't stay out too late, honey." There was worry in his mom's voice. "Be careful."

"I will. I just want some fresh air." Luke pushed his chair back, stood, and walked out of the room. He quietly left the house and sat down on the steps to the front porch. He watched the sky turn crimson as the sun slowly burned itself out behind the hills. A few stars ushered in the night, drawing the blackness of the eastern sky westward. Traces of orange and red were the only reminders of the sun when Luke ran his fingers through his hair, took a few deep breaths, and left the porch. His stride bespoke determination as he moved toward the old house. Breaching the threshold, he went directly into the back hallway. Luke was about to enter the last room guarded by the ornate doors when his curiosity for the plain wooden one overtook him. He pushed against it and found it shut as fast as it was before. He shook his head in bewilderment at the enigmatic door, whose purpose he had yet to discover. He then returned to the third door, with carvings of religious symbols and the plain, small building on its panels. With barely a pause, he opened the door and stepped through.

15

Friar Lewis

A voice floated out of the darkness, seemingly surrounding Luke with its quiet but firm tone. There was a subdued musical quality to the masculine voice that reached Luke as his eyes adjusted to the darkness around him.

"...and Father, forgive your humble servant. Strip me of pride and the frailty of my humanity. Give me strength to do your work faithfully. Grant me a measure of your Spirit to aid me in my mission. Lord, light my path, and guide me in your steps. Amen."

A shuffling noise came from Luke's right, indicating the owner of the voice was rising from his knees. The man moved across the room lighting a few weak candles, the sole source of light. The small wicks flickered to life revealing the form of the man with whom he shared the room.

He was plainly adorned, wearing a brown, hooded robe with a white rope cinched about his waist. His tonsured head bespoke someone who had dedicated his life to God's service. His dark hair was graying, giving the impression of a man moving past middle age. This stood in contrast with his frame, which was solid and his carriage regal, belying the true age of the man. His face was shaded from the dim candlelight, but Luke could see that the monk had a high forehead, a prominent nose, and a strong chin. His eyes appeared to be tired and dark.

The room was plain, as he knew it would be, furnished sparsely with a bed and a crude table and chair. The bed was roughly made and consisted of four short posts, a wide wooden plank on which to lie, and fresh hay to soften the bed. The table was against a wall under the solitary window. It appeared to be the monk's workstation. A small fireplace, a boiling pot, and a few cooking utensils rounded out the man's earthly possessions.

A soft darkness penetrated the window, chasing in the newness of the pre-dawn air. The starkness of the room struck Luke as he considered his own room back home. He pondered the dedication and fortitude required for such a life. The abject poverty, the crushing simplicity, shamed Luke. He was humbled by the sacrifices required to accept such a life. He lacked the simple, strong faith of this man and yearned for a measure of it himself.

"It is common for strangers to announce their presence before entering the home of their host."

The voice snapped Luke back from his thoughts. He turned his head toward the priest in stunned silence. Luke tried in vain to summon words. He felt bare and exposed, ashamed that he had been caught off guard.

"I am Friar Lewis. I keep this chapel and tend these grounds. What am I to call you?"

"My name is Luke." He paused for a moment to collect his thoughts. "I am sorry to come this way. I didn't mean to startle you."

"Worry not, Luke. You are welcome here. I will turn no stranger away. What is your purpose, traveler?"

Luke allowed a moment to pass before answering, scrambling to return an answer that did not sound insane. "I came here by chance," was all he could muster.

"There is no chance," he replied. "Do not discount God's providence. There is a purpose in everything. There are opportunities in everything. You are here for a reason." Lewis' eyes glowed with intensity. "I discern a plan behind your presence here, whether or not the plan is yours. But enough philosophizing." With that, the friar's eyes softened. "Be welcome. The sun is almost risen, and I have not yet broken my fast. Will you break bread with me?"

"Thank you," Luke replied, grateful that the man was willing to overlook his strange appearance.

"I am a man of humble means, but I will give you what I can. I only hope that my hospitality will compensate for any lack in physical sustenance." A twinkle entered Friar Lewis' eyes as he spoke. He seemed glad for some company.

Moving to his fireplace, Lewis picked up a plain wooden box from among the cooking utensils. He opened it to reveal the scant provisions that he had in his room. The two sat on the floor to share its contents.

Luke was just about to begin his meal when the friar interjected, "It would be an honor if you would allow me to bless this bread and the company with which I share it."

Feeling his face turn hot with embarrassment, Luke was glad that the friar had said it in such a way as to minimize his discomfort from the omission. "Yes, please," answered Luke in a chastened tone.

"Lord God, maker of heaven and earth," Friar Lewis began, "You are the All Knowing and All Seeing. You are the Giver of all Good Gifts, and for this I am gratefully bound to Your service. You have graced my life with Your presence and have brought about goodness where there was none. You have lightened my burdens and have given me my portion. But this portion was not meant to be hoarded, Lord. It is this I wish to share in whatever fashion I may with this solitary traveler. Father, sustain us with Your bounty and bring health from this meal. Give me strength to accomplish my purpose this day and allow Your light to shine through me to Luke, my companion. In the blessed name of our Holy Savior, Amen."

Luke felt moved by the earnestness of the prayer. The words seemed to flow from the soul of the speaker with a blinding faith. There was not a shadow of doubt in the prayer, not a modicum of confusion regarding his calling. As the echoes of the words died in the room, Friar Lewis raised his head and broke his bread, handing half to Luke. The two sat in silence breakfasting on dry bread and cheese. The portion was not large, but it was enough to assuage the hunger that had crept up on Luke.

"Please forgive me. I was not expecting a guest," Lewis noted, referring to the meager breakfast. "Now, for what purpose have you come today? Have you come to be healed?"

"No," Luke replied. "I don't need healing. I didn't know that I would end up here. I just happened upon this place." Luke purposefully kept his response vague, as he did not know how to explain the truth of his arrival. He was relieved when his reply seemed to suffice.

"This day is one of healing, and many have come for that purpose. Forgive me if I misread yours. Well," he said changing topics, "allow me to show you my ministry. I am a priest for the poor people of the land. I live here alone, tending a small chapel where these can come and worship. I tend a garden to brighten the eyes of those who visit and to fill the stomachs of the hungry." Lewis pulled himself to his feet and went to the door opposite where Luke had first entered. "Follow me, and I will show you the Lord's house."

Luke followed the friar through the door and into a dark room. Lewis lit a few candles mounted in sconces, brightening the space at the back of the chapel, which served as a transition from his living quarters to the small sanctuary. In the room, Luke found a small table with numerous vellum leaves written in a steady hand and roughly, but lovingly, illuminated. Several small wooden cups and bowls were neatly stacked on the floor under the table for use during the monk's holy duties. A wooden staff, a small wooden spade, and a spare robe were the only other items in the tiny room.

The friar lit two candles on the table, which were on either side of the vellum papers. The light brightened the color of the pages, adding a rich luster to the gold woven through the illumination. The picture on the first leaf caught Luke's attention, three empty crosses on a distant hill.

"Those are my most prized possessions. Those pages describe my light and life. Many years ago, a man once hung upon such a cross. But now it is empty, which is why we live." Friar Lewis' eyes filled with tears as he spoke, and he brushed his hand across the picture. There on his right hand was a ring that looked familiar to Luke. The ring caught the light of the candles and gleamed in the dim room. It was the identical ring to the one he had seen in his three previous journeys, the same one Luke bore on his hand.

"Friar Lewis, where did you get that ring?" Luke asked.

"This ring is a symbol of my family. It has been passed on from generation to generation and will continue to be so."

Luke pressed further, "Please forgive my ignorance, but how will the ring pass on if you are a man of God?"

"You are astute beyond your years," he said with a soft, sad smile. "This is a pain I carry with me. Before the Lord claimed my life as His own, a child was borne to a wife that I took while I was on a long journey. She died in childbirth, and I left the child behind. I speak this to my shame…." He paused as if to gather courage, "I left the child behind to continue my journey. When I came to the Light and realized that my life was not mine own, I was many days journey away. I could not bring myself to return to him, so I sent trusted friends in my stead. They found him and cared for him."

"Where is he now?" Luke wondered aloud.

"He is with my father. I have never seen my son but from a distance. Shame keeps me away from him. He is being raised well and is in the Lord's keeping. He has more than I could ever offer him. However, I fear I have sinned against him by staying away for so long. On the morrow, I will journey to my father's home to present my son with the ring. I know not how many years I have yet upon this earth, and I do not want death to take me before I present this to him." He waved his hand, as if could brush away painful memories. "But these people await my help, and I should not keep them waiting. I would enjoy your company while I pay my penance." Friar Lewis led Luke through the room and out a door on the end of the left-hand wall. The scene that opened before him almost took his breath away.

The chapel had rough, wooden floors, a small, vaulted ceiling and exposed timber trusses. The wooden walls had three small, glassless windows on either side. Plain iron sconces were mounted between the windows, holding three candles each. A small wooden platform, stretching out barely four feet, stood in front of them. It held a small altar, on which sat a miniature wooden cross bespeaking the simplicity and honesty of this place of worship. The light of the rising sun was breaking through the windows in the eastern wall, casting nearly horizontal beams into the interior. The room could not have been more than fifteen feet wide and thirty feet long.

Despite the hallowed feel of the simple chapel, it was not the building that struck Luke. It was the people. The church was filled with peasants. The only place people were not found was upon the platform. Nearly fifty men, women, and children had crowded the room in the predawn morning awaiting the coming of Friar Lewis. They were filthy and loathsome, filling the church with a stench. A wave of disgust washed over Luke as this unaccustomed sight presented itself.

"Friend Luke, this is the Lord's chapel, and this is my ministry. It shames me to speak of it, but I will not allow my pride to keep you in ignorance. Many years ago, I sinned in such a way that caused destruction to one very close to me." Friar Lewis paused as tears welled up in his dark eyes. He seemed to age a little just in the telling of the story. "But the Lord, in His infinite wisdom, has used my sin for His glory. Once a year, the Worker of Miracles blesses me with a healing gift. This blessing is also my penance, as it causes me pain." He lifted his hands, palms up, out in front of him. A tiny pinprick of red showed in the center of each palm, as blood slowly seeped out of some hidden wound.

The meaning of what Luke was seeing staggered him. His knees nearly buckled as awareness illuminated his mind like the sunlight illuminating the chapel. This was the very same Saint Lewis of which Princess Alexis spoke. He had figured her tale for a legend, but here was the embodiment of that legend, and Luke was present for his day of penance. With bated breath, he anticipated the scene that was about to unfold in front of him.

The friar stood for one moment more on the platform considering the seekers that were before him, some standing, some crouching, some lying down but all wracked with illness. Moving his lips in silent prayer, he descended into the crowd. Luke feared that the people would rush upon him, but they all stayed, waiting for their turn. They knew him, and they knew that no one would be missed. Friar Lewis cared for the people. They were his ministry, his mission, his life. They represented God's forgiveness in his life.

"Bring forth the children." Lewis' voice boomed with authority that none in the room dared deny.

16

The Healing

The crowd parted to make way for the children who were present. Shuffling feet and moving bodies were the only noises in the chapel. None of the peasants spoke a word. They were mute, in deference and respect to the monk. He was their hope, their healer from God, and this place was sacred to their simple souls.

Eight children were brought forward. Some were infants, whereas others seemed to have nearly fifteen years on the earth.

"Please, bring me the babes. It is them who the Lord loves. To such as this, His kingdom belongs."

With that utterance, a young mother, not yet eighteen, brought forth a gnarled baby boy. The infant was only six days old and growing weaker by the day. His face was misshapen with a cleft palate, and a riven lip. He was flush with fever. His left hand was withered, his twisted fingers shriveled and knotted on his disfigured hand. The body of the baby was bent, his crooked spine rendering his form limp. A soft whimper escaped his lips, springing tears from his mother's eyes.

"Friar Lewis, I have seen you heal. I have faith in God's power through you. Please restore my son, else his life will soon be spent."

The friar tenderly picked up the child and, holding him in his arms, lifted the boy to the sky and voiced a solemn prayer.

"Lord of heaven, see this boy's life as precious. Use this humble vessel to impart your healing. Heal his body and claim his life as Your own. Cleanse any impurities in my heart this day and make me worthy. Amen."

Friar Lewis handed the boy to his mother, his exposed flesh smeared with the blood of the healer. The whimpering had stopped, and the baby appeared asleep.

There had been no voice from heaven, no blinding light, nothing that would indicate a divine act had just occurred. In fact, Luke was unsure that any act *had* occurred. His doubt did not last long, however, as the proud mother turned to the people to show her child. She held a beautiful, whole baby in her hands. His fresh face slept peacefully, and his perfect hands lay gently on his straight body.

Bright sunlight flitted into the chapel, casting a heavenly glow on the mother and child, which seemed to diffuse and spread to the four corners of the chapel, warming the air. The windows seemed too small to be allowing such light. The effect on Luke was staggering. Out of all the experiences he had survived in the rooms of the old house, this was the most amazing. Luke felt frozen to his spot until the mother broke his trance by making her way out of the church. She stood in the doorway, tears of joy glinting in her bright eyes.

"God bless you, friar." With that, she turned and left.

The next child was a young girl, not yet two. She was brought forward by her father, who had a grim look of defeat on his face. His daughter looked like any healthy young child might, save for black, crusted holes where eyes should have been. The sockets were dry and cavernous. Her look was harrowing, and Luke dropped his eyes.

"Friar, I am no godly man. I have seen too much pain to have such faith anymore. I know not where to get the faith needed to heal my poor daughter."

"Ask and it shall be given unto you, my son" was all Lewis replied.

A single tear fell from the father's eyes as he dropped to his knees and buried his head in his hands. "God," he started with obvious pain in his voice, "I care not for myself, but give me that faith needed to heal my daughter…"

His broken voice trailed off as Friar Lewis bent to touch the girl. His hands reached for her face, dabbing a touch of blood on each of her empty sockets.

Her cracked eyelids closed for a moment before slowly flitting open. Pure azure eyes looked forth where barrenness had been before. Her gaze met Friar Lewis' and she smiled brightly before turning to her father. The man took his daughter's head in his hands and cried freely, releasing years of unbelief and bitterness. Father and daughter both left the chapel healed.

Lewis continued healing the remaining children, working wondrous miracles. With each wonder worked, Luke noticed a slow change in the friar. He seemed paler and weaker than earlier. The healing was drawing his strength. Whether it was from loss of blood or was part of his penance, Luke could not tell, but Lewis doggedly persisted, healing all who were brought before him.

After the children were healed and had left, Friar Lewis moved to the adults. But before he could begin his work on the rest of the peasants, a man burst through the door. He was regally dressed in bright, polished light armor, with a shirt of mail, silver greaves and gauntlets, and a matching helm. A shirt of fine blue fabric showed from under his mail and tanned leather pants were tucked behind the greaves. In his arms he held a maiden. Her broken form could not be hidden amongst the folds of her long, green dress. Blood trickled from her mouth as he entered the chapel.

"Desperation drives me to this door. I am a stranger passing through the land, and my lady was thrown from her mount. I fear she is at death's door, and I know not where to turn. My life is bound up in hers. I cannot lose her. I seek help from wherever it may come."

His imposing figure stood just inside the doorway. Light poured around him from the entrance to the little church, sunbeams seeming to bear him up before Friar Lewis.

"Stranger, seek, and you shall find. Your lady's healing is at hand." Lewis strode forward, placed his bloody palm on her forehead, and pressed his lips to hers. Slowly, he breathed into her, filling her lungs with air, then stepped back. She gasped, and her eyes shot open, wild with fright, but as her breathing steadied, her keen eyes calmed and cleared. The knight set his lady upon her feet, and she steadied herself with his shoulder, straightening her body and composing herself before addressing Friar Lewis.

"You have returned my life to me, and for that I will always be indebted to you." With an endearing smile, she kissed his forehead gratefully.

"This day I have found truth," the knight said, his voice cracking with emotion. "You have saved both our lives. How could I ever repay such a debt?"

"Serve God for the remainder of your life. That is all I ask," the friar replied warmly.

"That I will do. Farewell, and may God return blessings upon you." With that, the knight and his lady disappeared through the doorway.

Luke was moved at the passion of the knight and the strength of Friar Lewis. He continued to watch in rapt awe, as the man of God moved from the infirm to the crippled to the dying, healing and making whole. Maladies of every sort gave way before the touch of the penitent man. All the while, blood seeped from the friar's hands, draining his strength, while passing it on to others. With each healing, Lewis weakened. His shoulders were slumped, his regal stature seemed to be sinking into itself, giving way before the incessant trickle of blood.

Despite his wasting, Friar Lewis carried a look of purpose in his eyes. He moved with obdurate determination from person to person, healing disease, strengthening bones, sealing wounds, and giving hope. His weakening body was strengthening his spiritual objective. Each year, he recovered less and less from this day but drew closer and closer to his sense of purpose and the completion of his penance.

The sun had well passed its zenith and was beginning its slow descent by the time that Friar Lewis concluded the healing. His face was wan and weary. His body drooped under his brown robe, and his brow glistened with cold sweat as the last renewed body left the small chapel.

The departure of the last of the peasants snapped Luke out of his trance. He realized that he had not even left the platform, standing for hours, transfixed by his witness of the miraculous. He had experienced a display of incredible power, and even he felt drained after it was all over. He slowly stepped off the dais, as if he did not know what to expect from the ground underneath him. Making his way to the monk, he stood in silence, content to stand in awe near this holy man.

"Luke, come close, and lend me your shoulder. I feel as if *I* may be in need of some healing after this day," Friar Lewis whispered with a tired smile. "Help me outside. There is a bench near the chapel doors. A repose will help me gather my strength."

Finding their destination, a tired Friar Lewis plopped on the bench, leaned back against the chapel, and closed his eyes. The reddening sun cast a warm glow on the man's face, as his countenance relaxed, and he seemed to pass almost effortlessly into a peaceful slumber.

Luke joined him on the bench and took the opportunity to enjoy his surroundings. The chapel grounds were enclosed by a rough half-wall that demarcated the outer boundaries of the friar's garden. A deep green lawn established the inner boundary. Wildflowers grew in patches along the wall, creating intermittent splashes of color, balanced perfectly by small, flowering trees, some blooming pink, others white. A singular parcel of ground along the wall was churned and boasted rich, brown soil. Sustaining life coursed through the ground, enriching the food the friar had planted to keep his strength and those around him in need. He could work miracles only one day each year, but the ground was not so bound. The shoots of the vegetables had long since matured and were readying themselves for bearing fruit.

"It is beautiful, is it not?" offered Friar Lewis without opening his eyes.

His speech startled Luke, as he thought the man was asleep. "It is beautiful. Do you tend it all yourself?"

A small smile parted his lips. "It is a strange question. It can be said, after a fashion, that I tend these grounds. It would be truer to say that these grounds tend to me, and the Creator tends the earth. All life flows from Him, and I am merely a recipient of His goodness." His eyes remained shut as he spoke, but the gentle smile did not fade from his lips. His color had returned, and he seemed to be slowly gathering strength from the sinking sun, the fresh air, and the tranquility of his environment. He lapsed again into silence, drinking in his surroundings.

Luke could not help but join the priest in a smile. He was moved by the wholesomeness of the scenery, the green of the grass, the color of the flowers, the warm glow of the sun, the soft warbling of the birds. He found himself believing that he could drift to sleep and be forever lost in the serenity he now felt. His muscles relaxed as peace enveloped him. It was balm to his conflicted spirit. The concerns he brought with him from his time were floating away with the soft, summer breeze that rustled the leaves and caressed his skin.

"Luke, you are a young man to be traveling alone. You said that chance brought you here, but what brought you seeking?"

Friar Lewis' voice pulled him back to alertness. He was unsure of his answer and tried to walk a fine line between truth and obscuring the details of his situation.

"I recently discovered some difficult news and didn't know how to handle it. I wanted to escape for a while so I wouldn't have to think about it."

"Ah," Friar Lewis mused. "You seek solace in escape. Experience has taught me that escape is a false friend. Truth is the foundation of a holy life. Truth is like a door; avoiding it will shut you out. But knock, and it shall be opened unto you. Truth can be difficult, but, like a door, it always provides a way through. Strengthen yourself and return to your place. You will find what you need to overcome what stands in your way."

"I sure hope so," was all Luke could muster. The early evening sun and pleasant surroundings were again lulling him into a peaceful repose. The two figures rested on the bench for nearly an hour, neither asleep nor fully awake.

In the ebb of the setting sun, the trees and the half-wall cast long shadows on the lawn around the building. Lewis and Luke focused their consciousness, stood, and silently returned inside the church. Luke stood watching the priest slowly make his way to the front. The simple beauty of the little chapel struck Luke anew, almost moving him to tears, as he considered the humble friar, his miraculous work, and the soft remnants of the sinking sun warmly illumining the interior.

He took a deep breath, swallowed hard, and quickly caught up to the friar as he mounted the chancel at the front of the church. They proceeded into the small hallway and the friar's private quarters.

"Friend, you have seen what few hale persons have witnessed, but I am grateful for your company. As the years pass, the difficulty of this day increases."

"I'll never forget what I've seen today. I admire you for your dedication to these people. I don't know how to thank you for taking me in."

"You honor me with your presence and by accepting my humble hospitality," returned Lewis, with a warm but tired smile. "You are welcome to sup with me and remain as long as you will."

It pained Luke, as he knew he would have to refuse. Leaving was not his choice in his other three adventures. He returned to his own time when he wanted to stay. Now, he had the choice to stay and wanted to but knew that he had to return.

"I can't stay. I would love to remain with you, but I must go back. I have learned a lot from you. Thank you for everything."

"May God bless your steps and guide you safely home, my friend."

Luke turned toward the door. The priest's voice still lingered in his ear as he slowly stepped across the threshold, entering uneventfully back into the familiar hallway of the old house to his own time.

17

An Accident

Luke stood in the hallway for a short time, fighting back tears. Looking at the doors in turn, he thought of what each one had brought him. He had witnessed the death of a noble race behind the first door, was devastated to leave Ayne in his moment of need. The second door offered some hope for Ayne, as his legend had been passed down for generations, and his family ring had found its way onto Declan's deserving hand. Despite his desire, Luke was unable to protect Declan's family and found himself back in the old house. Upon entering the third door he had met a princess in her struggle to protect her realms from greed and selfish ambition, once again lighting the fires of hope for the lineage of Ayne. The fourth door opened a world of beauty and sickness juxtaposed and reconciled through the work of a remarkable friar. Luke felt like nothing he had experienced in his life had prepared him for the adventures he had in this house. He knew he could not return to the worlds behind the doors he had already opened. There was yet one door that he had been unable to breach. A door vastly different from the ones he had experienced. The door was humble and unremarkable and provided no obvious way to open it.

Luke knew that if he was going to find a way back into the world beyond these doors, he would have to find a way to open the final one. However, he realized that this one might be the last portal to other lands, possibly signaling the end of his amazing adventures. Despite this knowledge, he was determined to find a way through the final door.

Walking over, Luke placed both hands on the door and gave it a stiff push. It didn't budge. He tried to fit his fingers into the space between the door and the frame, attempting to pull it open but with no luck. He took a few steps back and tried to move the door with his momentum but only bruised his shoulder. Luke knelt in front and slipped his fingers underneath, but the door was so thick that he could not feel the other side.

His emotional state was such that he could not abide much frustration, and he left the door to itself. He shook off his sadness, missing all those he had met behind the doors and left the house in time to see the last stars struggling to illuminate the lightening sky. The sun was still below the horizon, but it was making its presence felt already by casting a warm, red hue where the sky met the land. Luke did not want the sun to find him outside, nor did he want his parents to find that he had not been in bed all night. He quickly went into his house and up to his room. The thought that he might not return to another realm, should he be unable to find the way to open the last door, began to creep over him. His knees weakened, and he crumpled onto his bed. The cumulative emotion from all his experiences washed over him. Sobs shook him until he was comforted in the arms of sleep.

It was early afternoon when Luke drifted out of sleep and sat up in his bed, having slept heavily through the morning. The emotion of the previous night was spent, and he laid back against the headboard, closing his eyes and enjoying the warmth of the sun coming through his window. He found himself drifting back to sleep, but his desire to try to find a way through the last door overwhelmed his sleepiness. He rose from bed and descended the stairs, attempting to locate the whereabouts of his parents.

"Mom…Dad…," Luke called out. There was no answer.

"Hello," he called but with no response. He entered the kitchen to find a note left on the table:

Your father and I have gone into town to do some shopping. I'm
 not sure what time we'll be back, hopefully in time for supper.

There are some leftovers in the fridge. Help yourself for lunch.
See you soon.
Love,

Mom

Luke took his mother's advice and lunched on the leftovers. He knew that he would need his strength to complete the project he had planned for today; he was determined to open the last door. He cleaned up from his short meal and went to the garage to look through his father's tools. With no clear plan, he looked around for what would most likely fulfill his purpose.

He went directly to his father's workbench, hoping to find the tools that would help him in his endeavor. Armed with a crowbar, a sledgehammer, and a chainsaw, he left the garage. Luke's intention was not to damage the door, but he was determined to open it. Striding out of the garage and into the old house, he flung open the front door, walked through the front room and into the back hallway. At the last door, he set down the tools. As he pondered the task before him, he itched with the desire to open the door. He wanted, he needed, to know that he could get behind it.

In truth, Luke did not truly feel the need to enter the door immediately; rather, it was the fear that he would never be able to find a way to open it that drove him to such lengths. He picked up his first tool, the crowbar, and proceeded to work. He wedged the curved end into the space between the door and the jamb, gave it an extra push to secure its place, and began to pry. Luke's muscles strained, he groaned from exertion, and small beads of sweat began forming on his forehead. His legs and core focused their flexed strength on loosening the door from its place. This continued for upward of thirty seconds before Luke's white knuckles released their grip on the bar. His hands were shaking, and his fingers felt locked into place. He slowly flexed his hands and wiped his moist forehead with his sleeve. The door had not budged. Luke pursed his lips with grim determination and tried once again with similar results.

Luke removed the crowbar and slipped his fingers into its place and felt the door. There were no splinters and no dents. All his efforts had produced no effect. He sat back against the wall to consider his situation, confounded that this door could be so immovable. He was loath to use the other tools he had brought, but he could see no other option. Rising, he took hold of the sledgehammer and prepared himself mentally to damage this mysterious door. It was not a task he relished, but he felt it was something he must do. He tried the weight of the hammer in his hands, adjusted his grip, swung the hammer back, and brought it crashing down.

The sledgehammer thudded to the floor, and Luke clasped his stinging hands together between his knees, as he bent over in pain, his arms throbbing up to his elbows. The door withstood the hammer as if it had been a mere stick. If the door had vibrated from the blow, it had stopped by the time the stinging had subsided in Luke's hands. He did not repeat the performance. Throwing the sledgehammer aside, frustration pulsed through his veins. He had not expected such resistance from this door. This was beyond reckoning and Luke could not fathom the strength behind it. He decided to let his hands fully recover before trying the chainsaw.

It took several minutes before the pain had drained from his arms, and he took up the saw. Steeling himself against the door, he was ready to make it a pile of splinters to get through. He wiped his forehead again, and dried his palms on his pants, one at a time, to make sure his grip did not slip. Then he primed the saw, throttled it, and pulled the cord. The chainsaw sputtered to life for an instant before dying. Luke yanked the cord several more times, not achieving the success of the first pull. He primed it again and pulled the cord half a dozen times before setting the saw down. The gas tank was full; he knew his father had just used the chainsaw several days before with no problems. So, he primed the saw again and pulled the cord. Still, no success. The combination of anger and frustration overtook Luke, and he yanked the cord back more than a score of times in rapid succession until he was out of breath and his arm was too tired to pull again immediately with good force.

Luke slammed the chainsaw down, gritted his teeth, ran his fingers through his hair, and dug his fingers into his scalp. Standing against the wall, he slid down until he was sitting on the floor, pulled his knees close to him and cried into them. The tears flowed freely, draining his anger and frustration, exhausting his emotion and strength. He knew no other way to enter the room. The door would not budge. There were no windows to the room and no other door. It was sealed off from all entrance. Luke despaired of any way in and slowly raised himself to his feet. Forlorn, he collected the tools and left the house.

His defeated stride stood in sharp contrast to the determined steps he had displayed less than half an hour before. Despite his slow steps, he soon reached the garage and deposited the tools back in their place. Inside the house, he sat down on the couch in the living room.

It was not long before he was up pacing. He was anxious for his parent's return. Understanding that their return would not help him get the door open, at least he would not be alone with his thoughts and frustration. His pacing served to keep his despair at bay. Restlessness consumed him for several hours, before he realized that the day was not nearly as bright as it had been. The sun was going down, and it was early evening. He thought his parents would have returned by now, but the letter was ambiguous on this point. He picked up his phone to call his parents' cell, when there was a knock at the front door.

The knock seemed very strange to Luke, as there were few visitors to his out-of-the-way home. In fact, it had been over a month since they had received anyone. Luke quickly went to the door, glad for any diversion from his pacing. He opened the door, and before him stood a policeman.

"Are you Luke Detter?" the policeman asked.

"Yes, I am. What can I do for you officer?" Luke asked quizzically.

"Are these your parents?" With the question, the officer produced file photos of his parents and presented them to Luke.

"Yes, they are. What's going on here? Has something happened to them?" Concern crept into Luke's voice.

"I am very sorry to be the bearer of this news, young man. Your parents were killed in a motorcar accident today. I am so sorry."

"No! This can't be right. They were just out shopping! There must be some mistake." Luke's voice cracked with emotion.

"I am sorry. Really, I am. I know that this is a difficult thing, to lose your parents, but I am going to need you to come with me to identify them. Is there anything that you need before we leave?"

Luke stood in stunned silence considering the possibility that the man was right. The policeman stepped aside and motioned Luke through the door. He walked in a daze to the car and entered. The policeman's words replayed in his head, and he began to sob. The sound of the car pulling from the driveway was the last thing he remembered until he arrived back at his home that night. He must have done what was necessary, because he found himself delivered to his front door by the same officer a few hours later. Luke heard vague chatter about phoning his closest relative and a car coming in the morning, but none of this mattered anymore. He slowly entered his home, now acutely aware of its emptiness.

In a daze, he kicked off his shoes and trudged up the stairs. Upon reaching his bedroom, he gazed at his parent's open door, grief welling up in his chest, constricting his throat. Tears flowed afresh from his eyes, as he entered his room and collapsed on his bed. Sorrow shook his frame, as his heart desperately cried out for his parents. Suddenly, his adoption did not matter anymore. They were his parents. They had always been his parents, and now he would never see them again. The throbbing headache, the violent sobbing did nothing to abate his tears. Sleep soon took him from his grief, although it was a fitful slumber.

Images of his parents floated before him. Happy moments played in his dreams, but his parents were always out of reach. They would not or could not respond to him, would disappear when he tried to touch them. Grief found him even in his sleep, and soon his parents were gone also in his dreams. It was not long, however, before he was joined by another figure.

Friar Lewis appeared before him every bit as real as when Luke had witnessed his miraculous healings. His head was tonsured, his body cloaked in coarse brown cloth, cinched in the middle with a white cord. However, there was something different about his appearance. It only took Luke a moment to notice what it was. The weariness his body wore and fatigue in his spirit was gone. His eyes were bright and his shoulders strong.

In Luke's dream, the two were back in the small chapel. They were alone. The sunlight from the windows filled the small room with a warm glow that enveloped the two friends. There was no sound coming from without the chapel, but the air within vibrated with a soft tone, almost as if a harp had been plucked, resonating into eternity. The atmosphere seemed viscous, almost like Luke was suspended in air. It was incredibly peaceful and comforting.

Despite the fear of shattering the peace with the sound of his own voice, he decided to address his companion.

"Friar Lewis?" Luke's voice had an odd quality to it, like it only existed in his mind and had not penetrated his tranquil surroundings.

The friar's response held the same quality. "Yes, my son?"

"How did I get here?" The words faded in his mind even as they were thought.

"You are dreaming," Lewis proclaimed. "I have been sent to guide your steps this night. You know all there is to know to achieve your goal, but your mind is clouded."

"I can't do it, Friar Lewis. I have tried, and there's no way through." Luke felt despair creep back over him.

"Think back to our time together."

At the cleric's prompting, waves of memories flooded Luke's mind. It was as if he was reliving his time with the friar, minute by minute. He remembered everything and began to realize the meaning behind his encounter with the holy man.

"Ask...," began Friar Lewis.

"...and it shall be given unto you," finished Luke.

"Seek...," Lewis continued.

"...and you shall find," Luke echoed.

"Knock..."

"...and it shall be opened unto you."

"Son, you have found your way. Go forth and do so."

With those words, the chapel faded, and Luke snapped into wakefulness. He jumped out of bed. Although it was yet night, there was no reason to delay what he needed to do.

18

Home

Excitement pulsed through Luke as he beheld the solution to his problem. His spirits were only slightly dampened by the thought that the solution seemed so simple. He quickly pushed the thought aside, placing his faith in the message given to him by Friar Lewis.

Luke was about to run out of his house and into the ancient one, when he stopped dead in his tracks. The journey that lay before him was unlike the other times. A surge of emotion came over him, as he realized that he had no intention of coming back to this place. With his parents gone, he had no desire to return. The thought of his parents brought with it a pang of grief, sapping him of energy, and bringing a momentary end to his excitement but not his determination.

Now with a more level head, he knew that there was much to do to equip himself for his journey. He had no idea what to expect on the other side of the door, and a flash of fear came and went as he thought about the foolishness of rushing into the unknown, leaving his home for good, unprepared. Luke tried to calm his rushing mind to consider what he needed to do.

Grabbing a backpack, he filled it with warm clothes, a knife, and a spare pair of shoes. He quickly stepped in the shower, trying to clean both his body and mind, wanting to rid himself of grief and grime. Luke emerged from the shower feeling better, donning some durable clothes and a pair of boots. The kitchen was his next destination as he filled his backpack with food.

As Luke stepped from the kitchen and into the living room, the darkness and the silence of the house oppressed him. The sun was still hours from rising, and he had not bothered to keep on any lights other than in the kitchen. Now that those had been extinguished, Luke felt acutely alone and exposed. Memories of his parents again begin to creep into his mind. He burst out of the house, as if leaving the house was tantamount to leaving his pain behind.

The night was crystal clear, the blazing stars charting their course across the ebony heavens. The cool air stroked Luke's face and hair, as he gazed at the stars. He felt a twinge of sadness, as he looked up at the sparkling sky. Maybe it was because he wondered deep down if it was the last time he would see it. He was still determined to open the door, but suddenly his urgency disappeared. It was almost as if he was a condemned man on death row, knowing the end was near and trying to savor every second of the familiar before it would be gone forever.

Luke stood for several more minutes gazing at the light descending from myriad after myriad of heavenly orbs before slowly moving on. Suddenly, the mundane details of his surroundings jumped out at him. He heard the calling of the birds in the distance. The swish of his feet over the grass caught his attention. He even bent down to feel the blades in his hands once more. *When was the last time I stooped to touch the grass?* he wondered to himself. The faint smell of salt from the ocean reached his nostrils, and he took a deep breath, filling his lungs.

Despite his lack of urgency, he soon reached the front door of the ancient structure and paused once more before entering. *Will this last door mean the end of my life as I know it? Would I ever see home or England again?*

There was a sadness that accompanied these questions. However, a tingling excitement also took hold of him, as he realized that he was planning to leave his life behind and enter the unknown.

His heart yearned for those left behind. He thought of Ayne and his impossible predicament. He prayed for the safety of Declan and his family, being forced to leave them in their moment of need. He missed Alexis and her regal youth. She was truly a jewel to be treasured. Possibly most of all, he coveted the presence of Friar Lewis. He had learned much through that remarkable man, the meaning of self-sacrifice and the goodness that can come from the work of a single person.

With all four of these friends on his heart, he entered the house for the last time. The prickling feeling of pins and needles washed over his body, such was his excitement as he entered the front room. He was struck afresh with the amazing handiwork that made the room look half forest. Remembering again his adventures with Ayne, Luke looked at his ring - the very same ring that he first saw upon Ayne's noble hand. He smiled to think that this treasure could have survived all this time and fallen into his hands. He thrilled at the thought that he might be a true descendant of the lost and noble race.

It was with a tear of reminiscence in his eye that he left the room and proceeded into the back hallway. He paused at each door as he passed, thinking back to his short but life-altering experiences in each. The first door on his left was the portal through which he had met Princess Alexis. He remembered the astounding story she relayed, in which he had first learned of Friar Lewis.

Luke turned to his right to gaze at the door that made Alexis' story a reality. Luke shook his head, still in disbelief of the miracles the friar had wrought, spending his very life essence helping the poor and the sick. Luke touched the door softly, tracing the carvings of the building and surrounding gardens. For a moment, he almost felt as if he was sitting outside the church with Lewis, basking in the evening sunshine, drifting in and out of a sleepy, peaceful consciousness.

At last, Luke moved on. He reached the room on his left, which had brought him to Declan. Declan had brought him his first hope that Ayne might have survived. That is where he first saw Ayne's ring on another's hand and when he was shown the likeness of Ayne's sword in the sky. Luke could think of no better way to honor the last of his noble race than to have his memory linked to the heavens, his story told in the stars.

Finally, Luke turned to the only door through which he had not ventured. He stood in wonder at the plain door that would not budge. It was inauspicious, to say the least, and was much less interesting than the others through which he had been. However, this one was proving to be the most mysterious. What must lie beyond this door that it would be sealed in such a way! A fleeting fear crossed Luke's mind that this door might not actually lead anywhere, just a quirk of the house with nothing but a wall behind.

Luke did not let the thought take hold, as he strengthened himself with his dream of the holy man, sent to give him the key through this door, proving impossible to open otherwise. He touched the door softly, feeling its rough imperfections and wondering anew at the mysteries that it held. Backing away from the door, he beheld it one last time, drinking in everything he could of his current life before it would change forever.

Awash with mixed emotions, Luke stood still, deciding which moment would be the last before leaving behind everything he knew. He was prepared to set aside the grief for his parents to permanently enter what awaited him on the other side of the door. Fear and excitement combined, making his stomach a knot of butterflies. He mourned his parents' passing but knew that it had given him the freedom to pursue this door and shut his old life behind him.

Luke decided that he had stalled long enough. With a mixture of loss and anticipation, he slowly stepped up to the door. He felt his heart pounding and his palms sweating. He took a few deep breaths to still his heart and wiped his palms on his pants. This was the moment he had been waiting for. If his experiences and feelings were a barometer for the truth, this was the culminating moment of his life. A sense of purpose overshadowed his nervousness, as he thought about his experiences and who he was. He was Luke, descendant of the last of a lost people, bearer of Ayne's ring, the discoverer of the magic locked in the ancient house, dreamer of dreams that not only led him to the house but provided him with the key through the last door. He was ready, ready to step across the boundary into the unknown and discover why he was chosen for this, ready to leave it all behind - cast it aside and step forward in faith. Raising his hand to the door, he took a deep breath, closed his eyes, and whispered the friar's words softly, "Ask, seek, knock," rapping on the door with his knuckles as he spoke the last word.

* * *

A gentle breeze surrounded Luke, swirling around him, coursing through him, seemingly bearing him up. The delicious air filled his lungs giving him a giddy, lightheaded feeling that was entirely pleasurable. The feeling of weightlessness crept upon him, almost like he was suspended in light, breathable fluid of an exquisite temperature and consistency. How long he was in such a state Luke could not discern. It could have been moments; it could have been days. Time seemed to blend and disappear. Thought followed suit, having lost all reference upon which to base what he was experiencing - seemingly limitless, pure, and wholly sensual.

Awareness began to dawn upon Luke, bringing him back to himself, almost breathless from his journey through the door. He found himself lying on soft, springy turf, and he quickly picked himself up in an effortless fashion. What surrounded him seemed incredibly familiar, yet from the memory of a distant dream.

Before him was what appeared to be a small chapel yard, lovingly tended and surrounded by a sturdy half-wall. As he turned around, gazing at his environs, remembrance began to come back him, and he was surprised that he did not know it at first. Yet how could he have known it. The chapel yard he remembered was but a poor substitute for what stood before him. It seemed like he had been viewing the world through a dirty, faded mirror and was only now allowed to look directly at the world and see it for what it was.

The intensity of the place struck him. The textures were so fresh, the sounds sharp and bright, the smells so intense, and the colors so full and pure. Luke wondered how anything had looked beautiful to him before. Having been awed by this world he had entered, he mourned the loss of the incredible timeless and weightless sensations he first experienced passing through the door. Then, like a song which has faded into the background, the thought of it brought the sensation back fully upon Luke. He then realized that it had never really left; it was blended into his total experience, providing the melody for the harmony of his surroundings.

Overwhelmed by his senses, Luke failed to perceive a figure moving closer to him. Luke started out of his reverie when a gentle hand was placed upon his shoulder.

"Friar Lewis!" The words escaped out of Luke's mouth almost before the thought had fully formed in his mind. The form now facing Luke was certainly familiar, but it was so changed that doubt began to crowd into Luke's mind.

"That I was and suppose I still am, although there is no need for friars here."

"No need?" Luke asked in surprise. "What about your ministry to the people of the land, your penance?"

"Son, the days of my penance are passed." He held out his fresh, unblemished hands. "There is but One who bears those scars, such as I am not fit to bear. Likewise, there are none here who need these hands for sustenance. All is good, all are well, and all is provided. There are none who are wanting in joy and fulfillment."

Luke felt a surge of happiness, as he looked upon a young, healthy, vibrant version of his friend. He seemed the embodiment of what humanity was meant to be. He matched the exact sentiment of his surroundings, overflowing with purity and perfection.

"Where are we?" queried Luke.

"We are home. This place is more home to us than any that we have ever experienced. This place was made for us and for our enjoyment."

"How is it that this was made for just us?"

The friar laughed good-naturedly, the ambient light highlighting the kindness in his face. "We are but a small portion of the hosts in this place. There are many who have come before and there are many who will follow after. But not many will come as you have. You are the terminus of a goodly race. You have been called hence out of a place where all remembrance and care for the purpose of your race has passed unheeded out of memory forever. The purpose of those magical people, once corrupted by humans, was almost completely destroyed. A single beacon, a reminder of what was and what could have been, survived from generation to generation. You had to know your past and embrace your legacy before you could pass hence. The last has finally been called home to a better purpose than was originally corrupted."

"What purpose?"

"The Elves' purpose on earth was to honor the Creator in their unity with the creation. Now their purpose is eternity with their Creator."

"So, am I dead?" Luke wondered aloud, concern creeping into his voice.

"No, friend. You are not dead. You have, in fact, just begun to live. What we formerly called life was merely a shadow, an imperfect form of what is here. You will understand more in time, for time is a plenteous resource here." With a knowing smile, Friar Lewis grasped the hand of his friend and led him out of the little churchyard, "Come, there is much to show you, and there are some who have been awaiting your arrival."